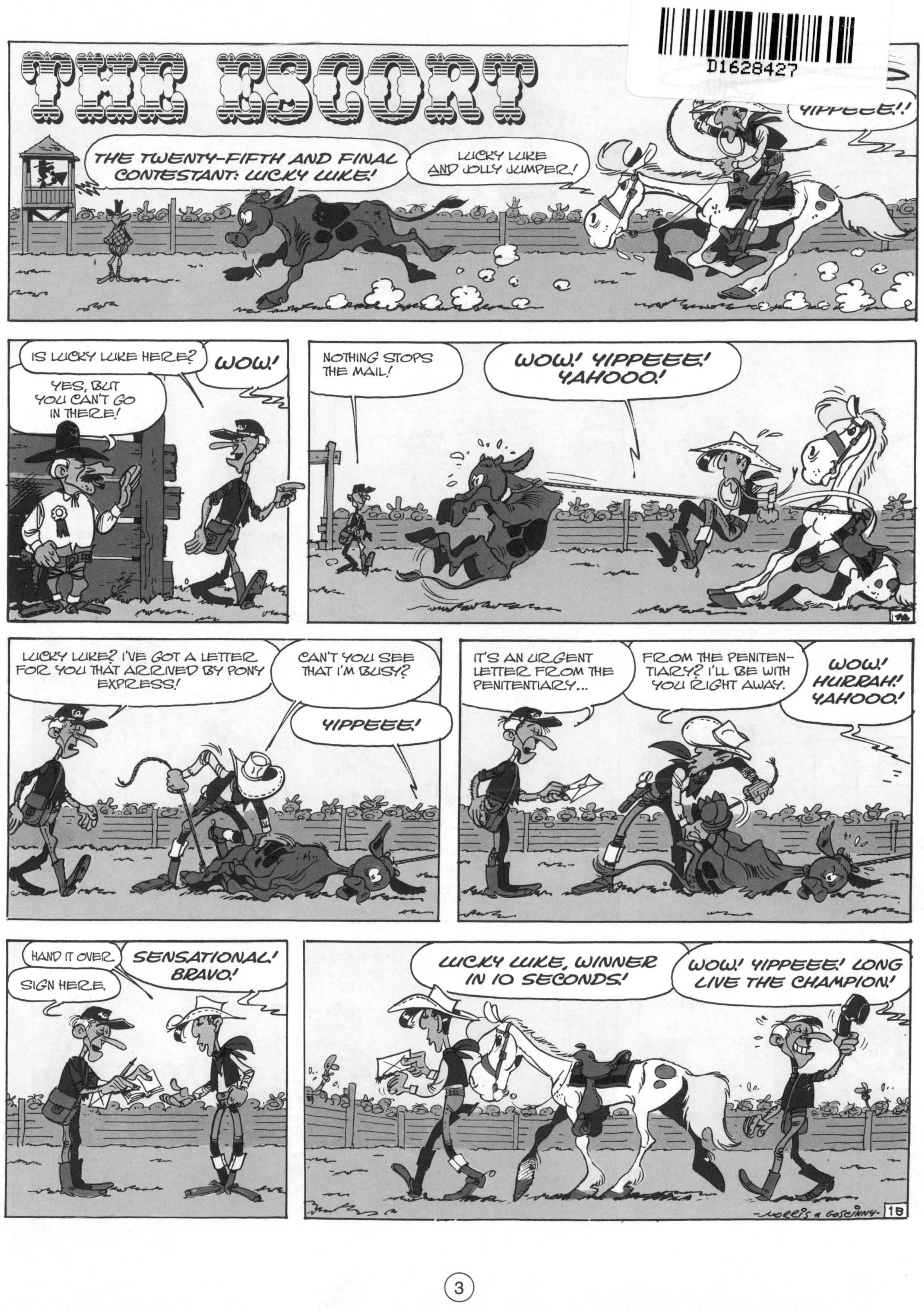
THE ESCORT
THE TWENTY-FIFTH AND FINAL CONTESTANT: LUCKY LUKE!
LUCKY LUKE AND JOLLY JUMPER!
YIPPEEE!!
IS LUCKY LUKE HERE?
WOW!
YES, BUT YOU CAN'T GO IN THERE!
NOTHING STOPS THE MAIL!
WOW! YIPPEEE! YAHOOO!
LUCKY LUKE? I'VE GOT A LETTER FOR YOU THAT ARRIVED BY PONY EXPRESS!
CAN'T YOU SEE THAT I'M BUSY?
YIPPEEE!
IT'S AN URGENT LETTER FROM THE PENITENTIARY...
FROM THE PENITENTIARY? I'LL BE WITH YOU RIGHT AWAY.
WOW! HURRAH! YAHOOO!
HAND IT OVER.
SIGN HERE.
SENSATIONAL! BRAVO!
LUCKY LUKE, WINNER IN 10 SECONDS!
WOW! YIPPEEE! LONG LIVE THE CHAMPION!

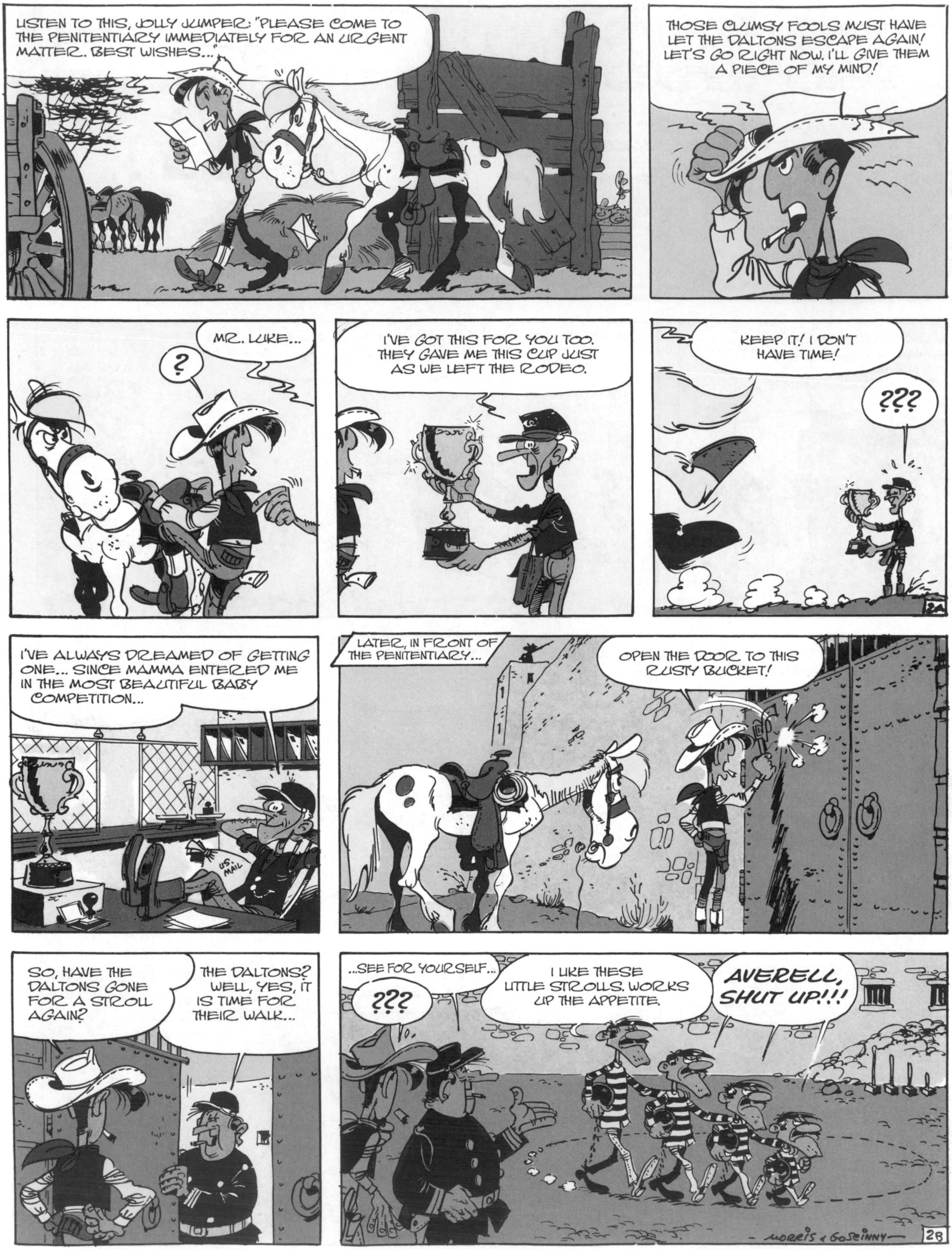

LISTEN TO THIS, JOLLY JUMPER: "PLEASE COME TO THE PENITENTIARY IMMEDIATELY FOR AN URGENT MATTER. BEST WISHES..."
THOSE CLUMSY FOOLS MUST HAVE LET THE DALTONS ESCAPE AGAIN! LET'S GO RIGHT NOW. I'LL GIVE THEM A PIECE OF MY MIND!
MR. LUKE...
?
I'VE GOT THIS FOR YOU TOO. THEY GAVE ME THIS CUP JUST AS WE LEFT THE RODEO.
KEEP IT! I DON'T HAVE TIME!
???
2A
I'VE ALWAYS DREAMED OF GETTING ONE... SINCE MAMMA ENTERED ME IN THE MOST BEAUTIFUL BABY COMPETITION...
U.S. MAIL
LATER, IN FRONT OF THE PENITENTIARY...
OPEN THE DOOR TO THIS RUSTY BUCKET!
SO, HAVE THE DALTONS GONE FOR A STROLL AGAIN?
THE DALTONS? WELL, YES, IT IS TIME FOR THEIR WALK...
...SEE FOR YOURSELF...
???
I LIKE THESE LITTLE STROLLS. WORKS UP THE APPETITE.
AVERELL, SHUT UP!!!
MORRIS & GOSCINNY
2B

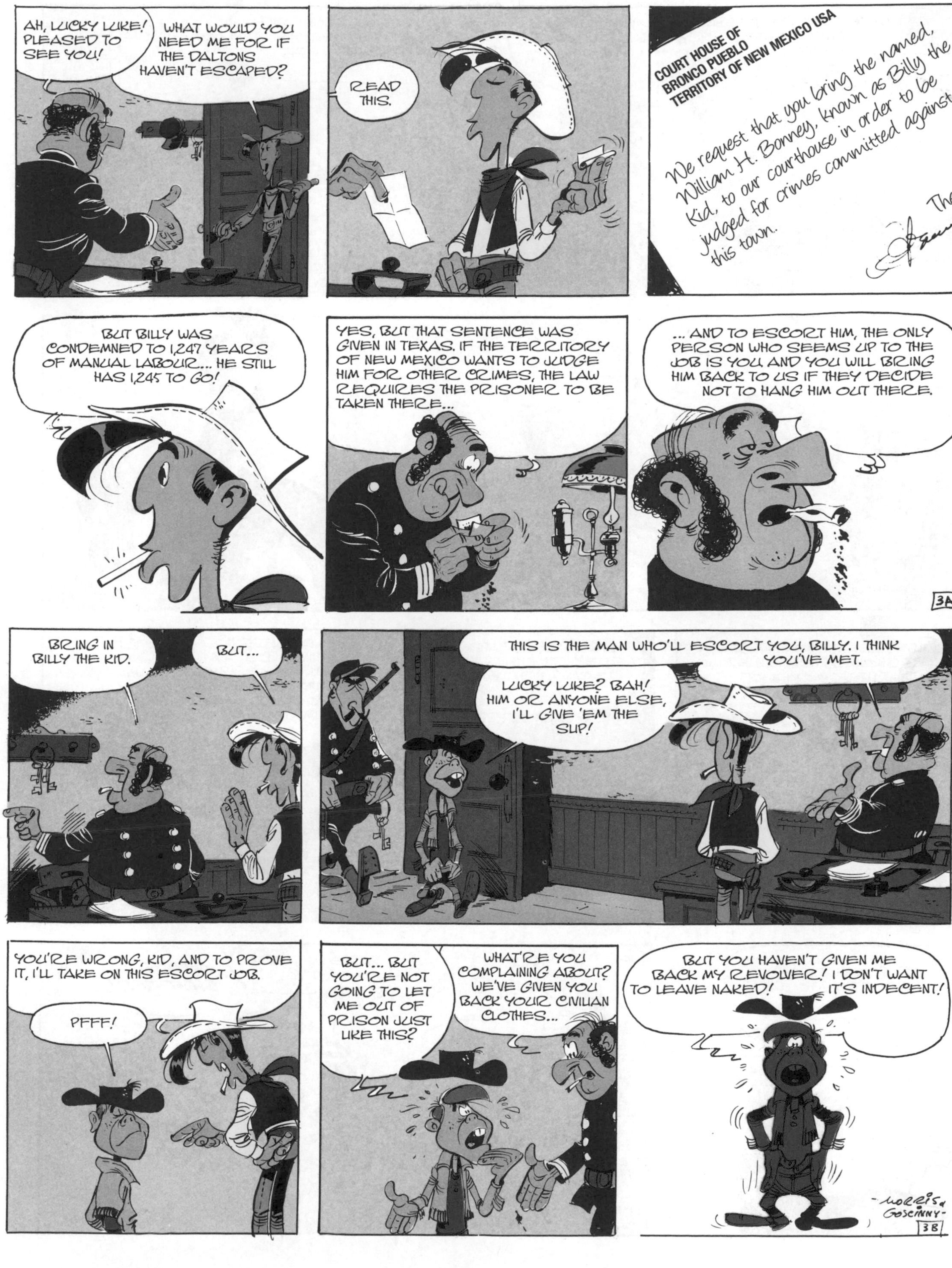
AH, LUCKY LUKE! PLEASED TO SEE YOU!
WHAT WOULD YOU NEED ME FOR IF THE DALTONS HAVEN'T ESCAPED?
READ THIS.
COURT HOUSE OF
BRONCO PUEBLO
TERRITORY OF NEW MEXICO USA
We request that you bring the named, William H. Bonney, known as Billy the Kid, to our courthouse in order to be judged for crimes committed against this town.
The
BUT BILLY WAS CONDEMNED TO 1,247 YEARS OF MANUAL LABOUR... HE STILL HAS 1,245 TO GO!
YES, BUT THAT SENTENCE WAS GIVEN IN TEXAS. IF THE TERRITORY OF NEW MEXICO WANTS TO JUDGE HIM FOR OTHER CRIMES, THE LAW REQUIRES THE PRISONER TO BE TAKEN THERE...
... AND TO ESCORT HIM, THE ONLY PERSON WHO SEEMS UP TO THE JOB IS YOU AND YOU WILL BRING HIM BACK TO US IF THEY DECIDE NOT TO HANG HIM OUT THERE.
BRING IN BILLY THE KID.
BUT...
THIS IS THE MAN WHO'LL ESCORT YOU, BILLY. I THINK YOU'VE MET.
LUCKY LUKE? BAH! HIM OR ANYONE ELSE, I'LL GIVE 'EM THE SLIP!
YOU'RE WRONG, KID, AND TO PROVE IT, I'LL TAKE ON THIS ESCORT JOB.
PFFF!
BUT... BUT YOU'RE NOT GOING TO LET ME OUT OF PRISON JUST LIKE THIS?
WHAT'RE YOU COMPLAINING ABOUT? WE'VE GIVEN YOU BACK YOUR CIVILIAN CLOTHES...
BUT YOU HAVEN'T GIVEN ME BACK MY REVOLVER! I DON'T WANT TO LEAVE NAKED! IT'S INDECENT!
-MORRIS et GOSCINNY-
38

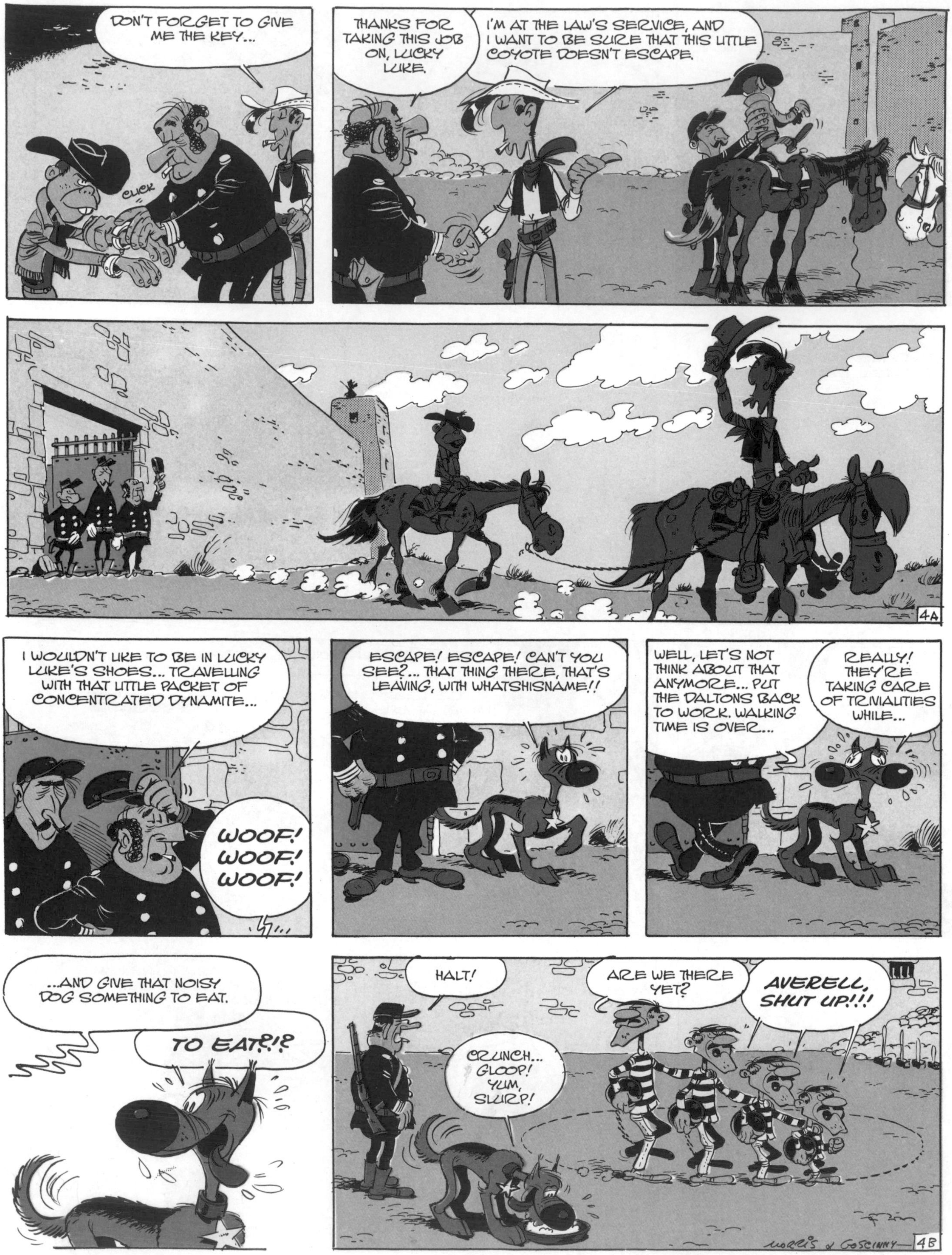
DON'T FORGET TO GIVE ME THE KEY...
CLICK
THANKS FOR TAKING THIS JOB ON, LUCKY LUKE.
I'M AT THE LAW'S SERVICE, AND I WANT TO BE SURE THAT THIS LITTLE COYOTE DOESN'T ESCAPE.
4A
I WOULDN'T LIKE TO BE IN LUCKY LUKE'S SHOES... TRAVELLING WITH THAT LITTLE PACKET OF CONCENTRATED DYNAMITE...
WOOF! WOOF! WOOF!
ESCAPE! ESCAPE! CAN'T YOU SEE?... THAT THING THERE, THAT'S LEAVING, WITH WHATSHISNAME!!
WELL, LET'S NOT THINK ABOUT THAT ANYMORE... PUT THE DALTONS BACK TO WORK. WALKING TIME IS OVER...
REALLY! THEY'RE TAKING CARE OF TRIVIALITIES WHILE...
...AND GIVE THAT NOISY DOG SOMETHING TO EAT.
TO EAT?!?
HALT!
ARE WE THERE YET?
AVERELL, SHUT UP!!!
CRUNCH... GLOOP! YUM, SLURP!
MORRIS & GOSCINNY
4B

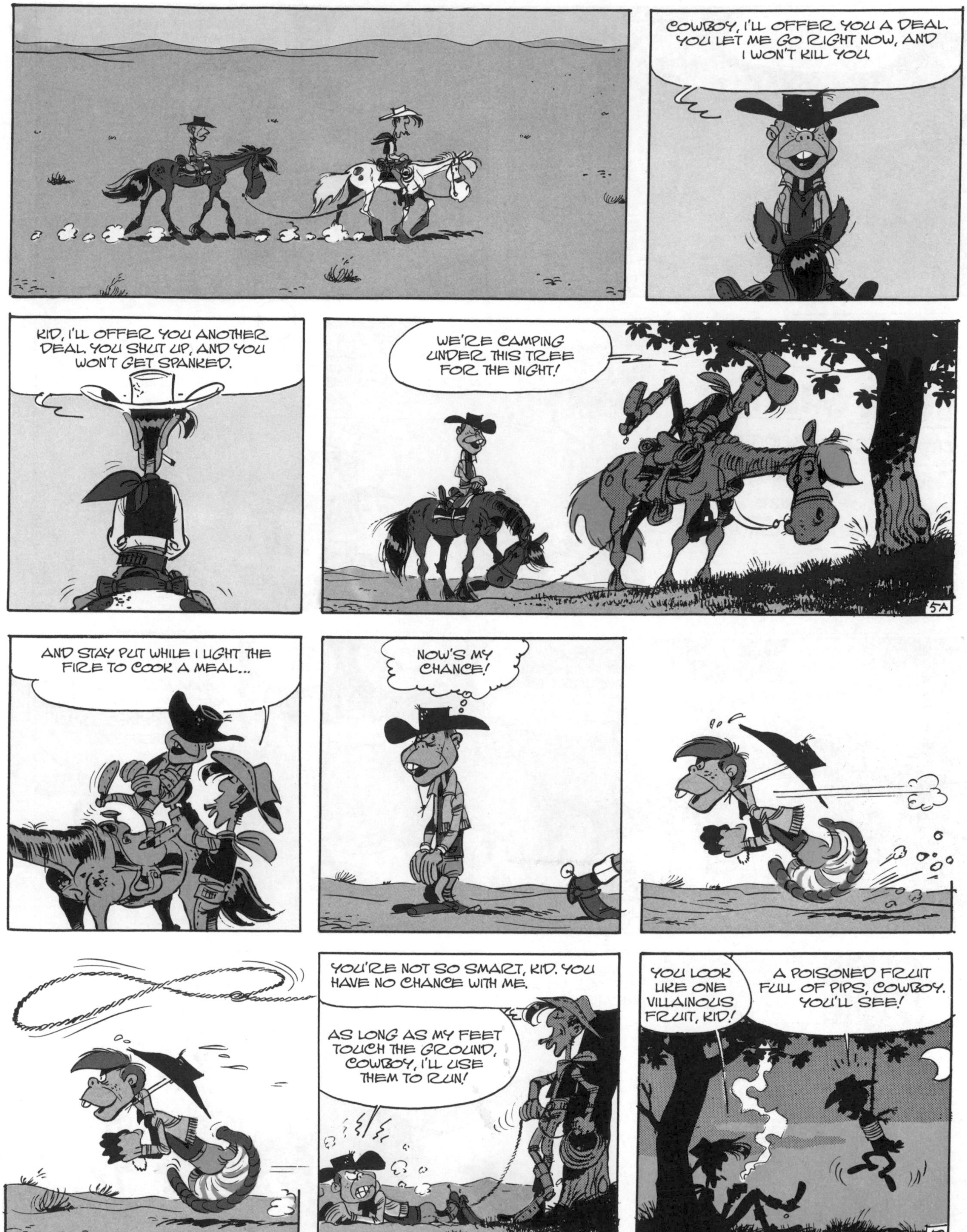
COWBOY, I'LL OFFER YOU A DEAL. YOU LET ME GO RIGHT NOW, AND I WON'T KILL YOU.
KID, I'LL OFFER YOU ANOTHER DEAL. YOU SHUT UP, AND YOU WON'T GET SPANKED.
WE'RE CAMPING UNDER THIS TREE FOR THE NIGHT!
5A
AND STAY PUT WHILE I LIGHT THE FIRE TO COOK A MEAL...
NOW'S MY CHANCE!
YOU'RE NOT SO SMART, KID. YOU HAVE NO CHANCE WITH ME.
AS LONG AS MY FEET TOUCH THE GROUND, COWBOY, I'LL USE THEM TO RUN!
YOU LOOK LIKE ONE VILLAINOUS FRUIT, KID!
A POISONED FRUIT FULL OF PIPS, COWBOY. YOU'LL SEE!
5B

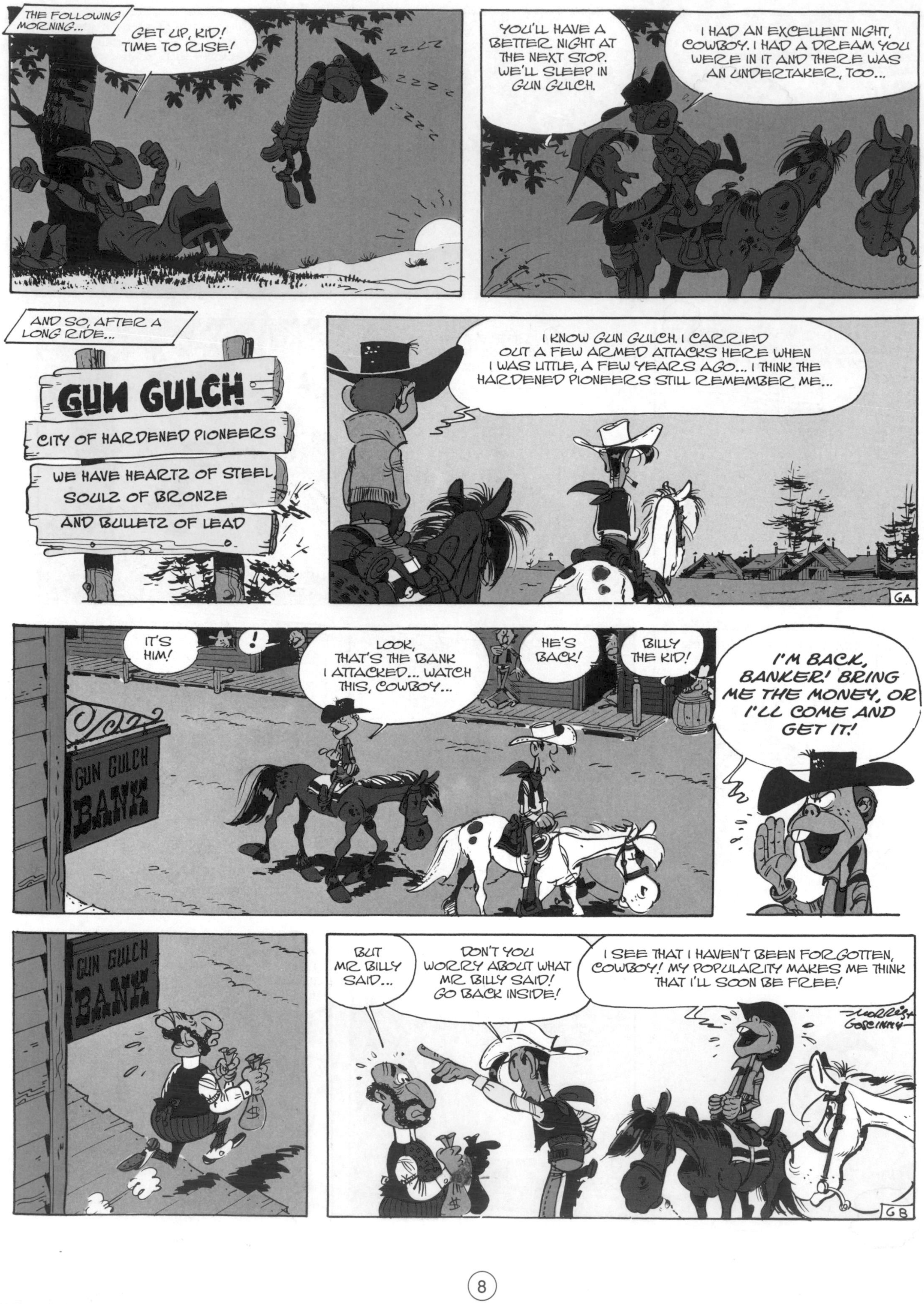
THE FOLLOWING MORNING...
GET UP, KID! TIME TO RISE!
ZZZZZ
YOU'LL HAVE A BETTER NIGHT AT THE NEXT STOP. WE'LL SLEEP IN GUN GULCH.
I HAD AN EXCELLENT NIGHT, COWBOY. I HAD A DREAM YOU WERE IN IT AND THERE WAS AN UNDERTAKER, TOO...
AND SO, AFTER A LONG RIDE...
GUN GULCH
CITY OF HARDENED PIONEERS
WE HAVE HEARTZ OF STEEL, SOULZ OF BRONZE
AND BULLETZ OF LEAD
I KNOW GUN GULCH. I CARRIED OUT A FEW ARMED ATTACKS HERE WHEN I WAS LITTLE, A FEW YEARS AGO... I THINK THE HARDENED PIONEERS STILL REMEMBER ME...
IT'S HIM!
!
LOOK, THAT'S THE BANK I ATTACKED... WATCH THIS, COWBOY...
HE'S BACK!
BILLY THE KID!
GUN GULCH BANK
I'M BACK, BANKER! BRING ME THE MONEY, OR I'LL COME AND GET IT!
GUN GULCH BANK
BUT MR BILLY SAID...
DON'T YOU WORRY ABOUT WHAT MR BILLY SAID! GO BACK INSIDE!
I SEE THAT I HAVEN'T BEEN FORGOTTEN, COWBOY! MY POPULARITY MAKES ME THINK THAT I'LL SOON BE FREE!
MORRIS GOSCINNY

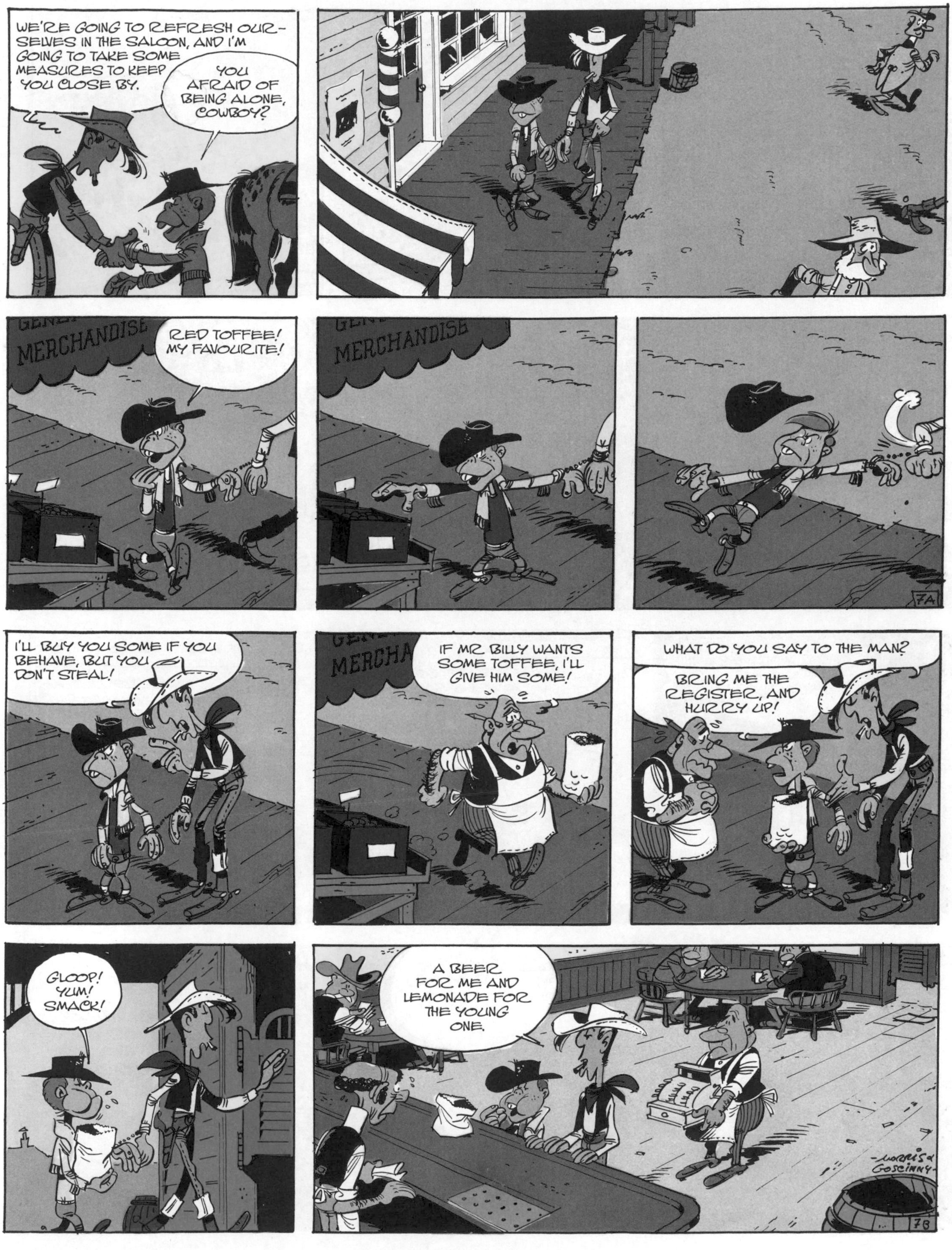
WE'RE GOING TO REFRESH OURSELVES IN THE SALOON, AND I'M GOING TO TAKE SOME MEASURES TO KEEP YOU CLOSE BY.
YOU AFRAID OF BEING ALONE, COWBOY?
GENERAL MERCHANDISE
RED TOFFEE! MY FAVOURITE!
7A
I'LL BUY YOU SOME IF YOU BEHAVE, BUT YOU DON'T STEAL!
IF MR BILLY WANTS SOME TOFFEE, I'LL GIVE HIM SOME!
WHAT DO YOU SAY TO THE MAN?
BRING ME THE REGISTER, AND HURRY UP!
GLOOP! YUM! SMACK!
A BEER FOR ME AND LEMONADE FOR THE YOUNG ONE.
MORRIS & GOSCINNY
7B

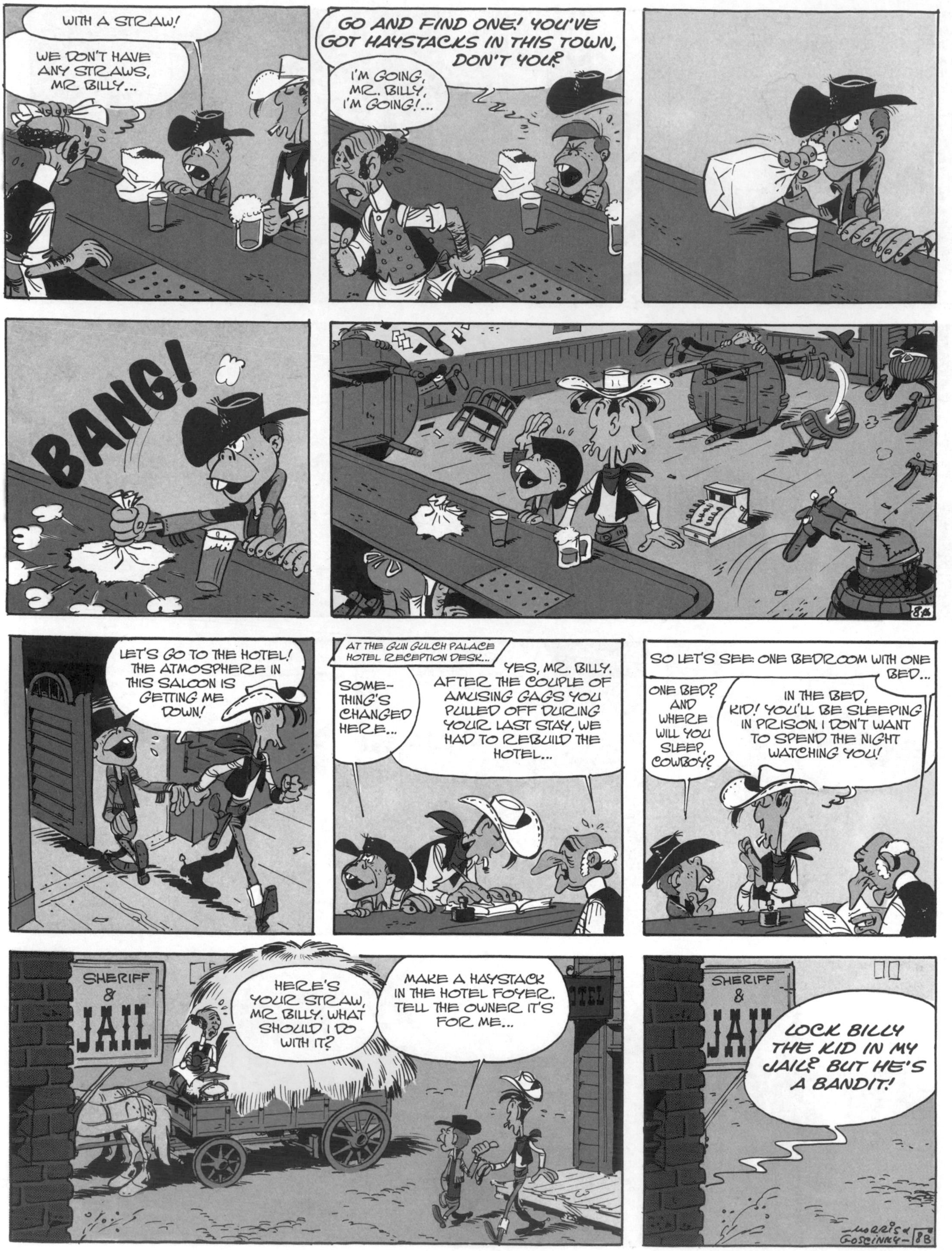
WITH A STRAW!
WE DON'T HAVE ANY STRAWS, MR BILLY...
GO AND FIND ONE! YOU'VE GOT HAYSTACKS IN THIS TOWN, DON'T YOU?
I'M GOING, MR. BILLY, I'M GOING!...
BANG!
LET'S GO TO THE HOTEL! THE ATMOSPHERE IN THIS SALOON IS GETTING ME DOWN!
AT THE GUN GULCH PALACE HOTEL RECEPTION DESK...
SOME-THING'S CHANGED HERE...
YES, MR. BILLY. AFTER THE COUPLE OF AMUSING GAGS YOU PULLED OFF DURING YOUR LAST STAY, WE HAD TO REBUILD THE HOTEL...
SO LET'S SEE: ONE BEDROOM WITH ONE BED...
ONE BED? AND WHERE WILL YOU SLEEP, COWBOY?
IN THE BED, KID! YOU'LL BE SLEEPING IN PRISON. I DON'T WANT TO SPEND THE NIGHT WATCHING YOU!
SHERIFF & JAIL
HERE'S YOUR STRAW, MR BILLY. WHAT SHOULD I DO WITH IT?
MAKE A HAYSTACK IN THE HOTEL FOYER. TELL THE OWNER IT'S FOR ME...
SHERIFF & JAIL
LOCK BILLY THE KID IN MY JAIL? BUT HE'S A BANDIT!
MORRIS & GOSCINNY 8B

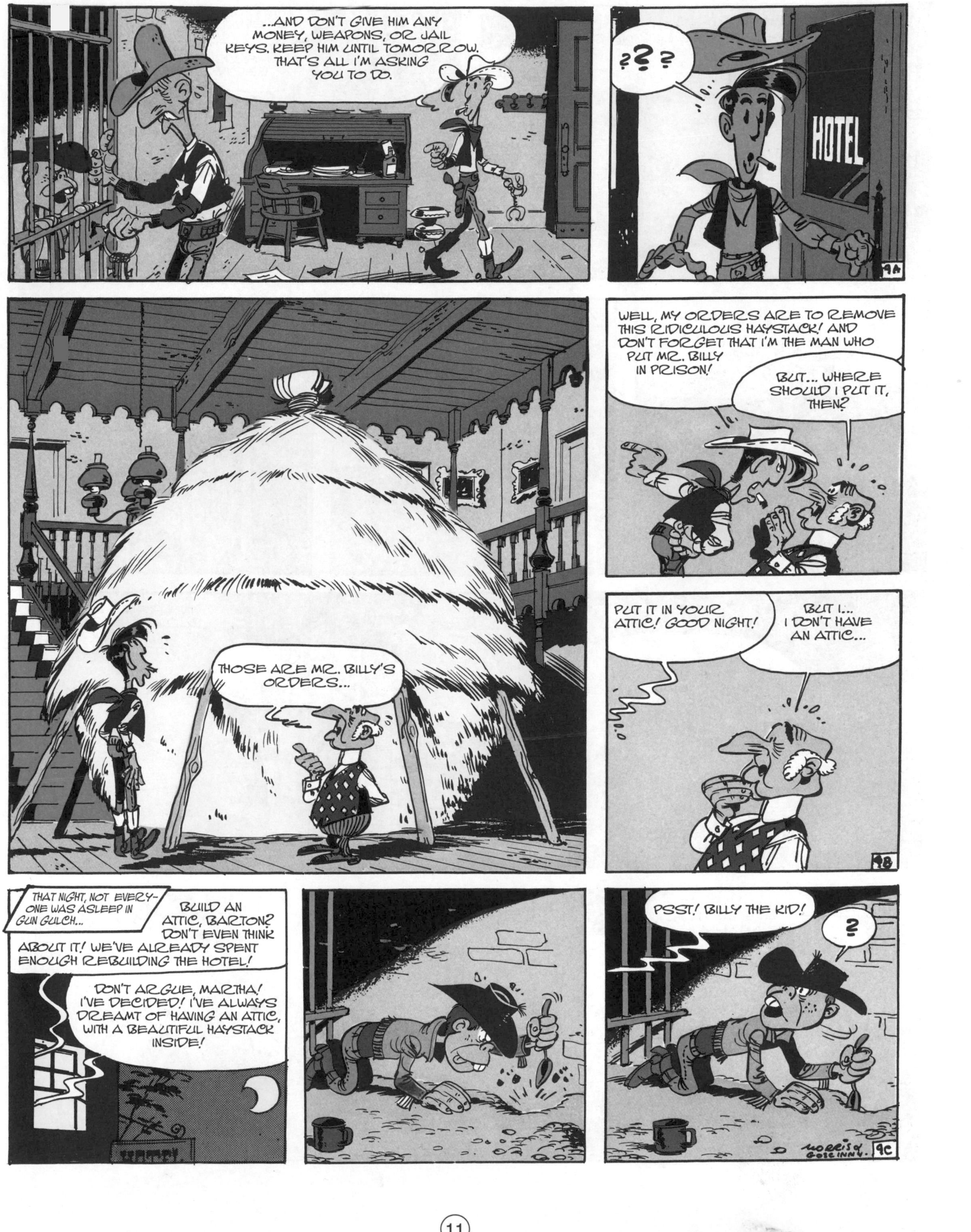
...AND DON'T GIVE HIM ANY MONEY, WEAPONS, OR JAIL KEYS. KEEP HIM UNTIL TOMORROW. THAT'S ALL I'M ASKING YOU TO DO.
??
HOTEL
9A
THOSE ARE MR. BILLY'S ORDERS...
WELL, MY ORDERS ARE TO REMOVE THIS RIDICULOUS HAYSTACK! AND DON'T FORGET THAT I'M THE MAN WHO PUT MR. BILLY IN PRISON!
BUT... WHERE SHOULD I PUT IT, THEN?
PUT IT IN YOUR ATTIC! GOOD NIGHT!
BUT I... I DON'T HAVE AN ATTIC...
9B
THAT NIGHT, NOT EVERYONE WAS ASLEEP IN GUN GULCH...
BUILD AN ATTIC, BARTON? DON'T EVEN THINK ABOUT IT! WE'VE ALREADY SPENT ENOUGH REBUILDING THE HOTEL!
DON'T ARGUE, MARTHA! I'VE DECIDED! I'VE ALWAYS DREAMT OF HAVING AN ATTIC, WITH A BEAUTIFUL HAYSTACK INSIDE!
PSST! BILLY THE KID!
?
MORRIS & GOSCINNY.
9C

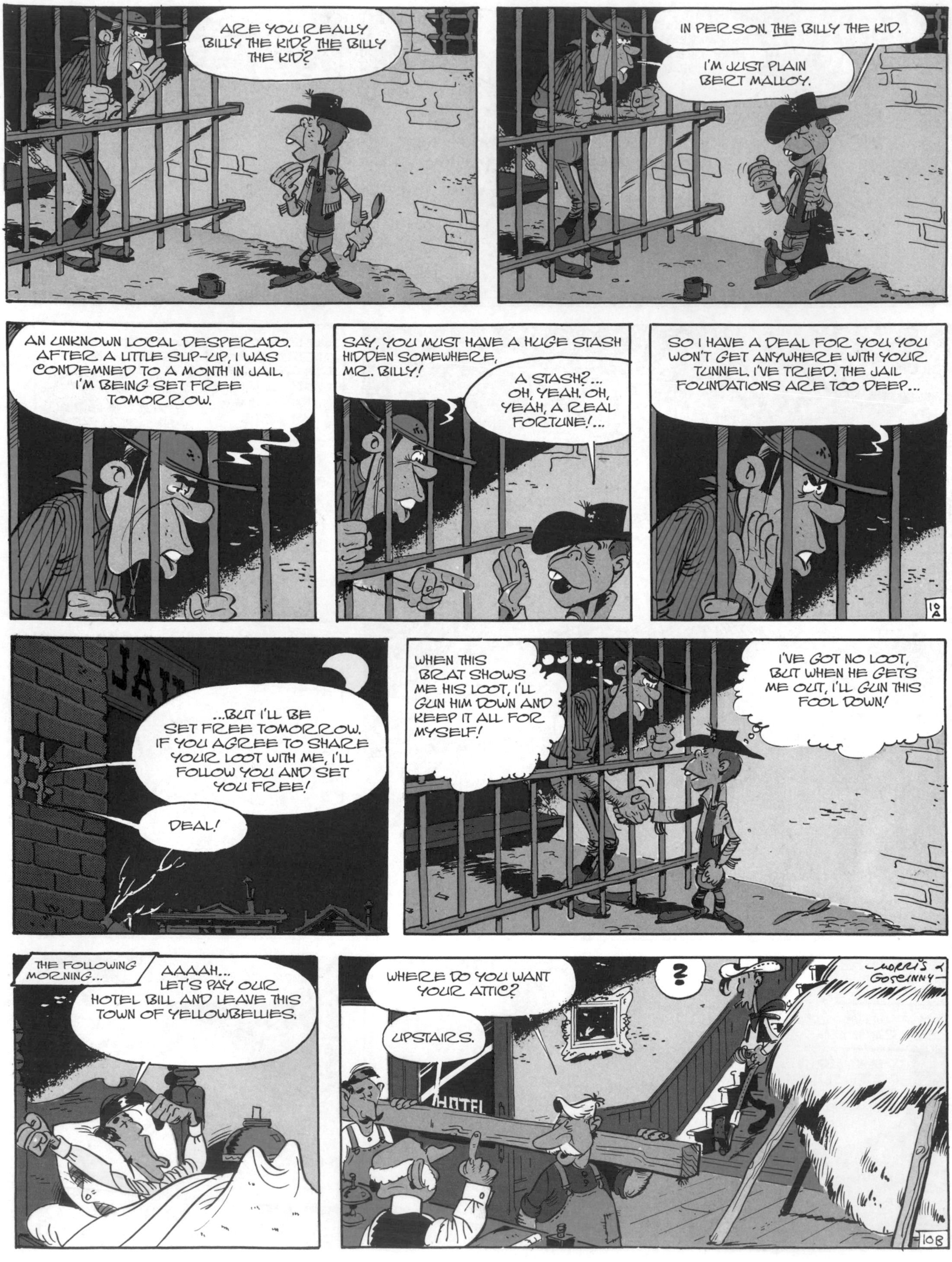
ARE YOU REALLY BILLY THE KID? THE BILLY THE KID?
IN PERSON. THE BILLY THE KID.
I'M JUST PLAIN BERT MALLOY.
AN UNKNOWN LOCAL DESPERADO. AFTER A LITTLE SLIP-UP, I WAS CONDEMNED TO A MONTH IN JAIL. I'M BEING SET FREE TOMORROW.
SAY, YOU MUST HAVE A HUGE STASH HIDDEN SOMEWHERE, MR. BILLY!
A STASH?... OH, YEAH. OH, YEAH, A REAL FORTUNE!...
SO I HAVE A DEAL FOR YOU. YOU WON'T GET ANYWHERE WITH YOUR TUNNEL. I'VE TRIED. THE JAIL FOUNDATIONS ARE TOO DEEP...
JAIL
...BUT I'LL BE SET FREE TOMORROW. IF YOU AGREE TO SHARE YOUR LOOT WITH ME, I'LL FOLLOW YOU AND SET YOU FREE!
DEAL!
WHEN THIS BRAT SHOWS ME HIS LOOT, I'LL GUN HIM DOWN AND KEEP IT ALL FOR MYSELF!
I'VE GOT NO LOOT, BUT WHEN HE GETS ME OUT, I'LL GUN THIS FOOL DOWN!
THE FOLLOWING MORNING...
AAAAH... LET'S PAY OUR HOTEL BILL AND LEAVE THIS TOWN OF YELLOWBELLIES.
WHERE DO YOU WANT YOUR ATTIC?
?
UPSTAIRS.
HOTEL
MORRIS & GOSCINNY

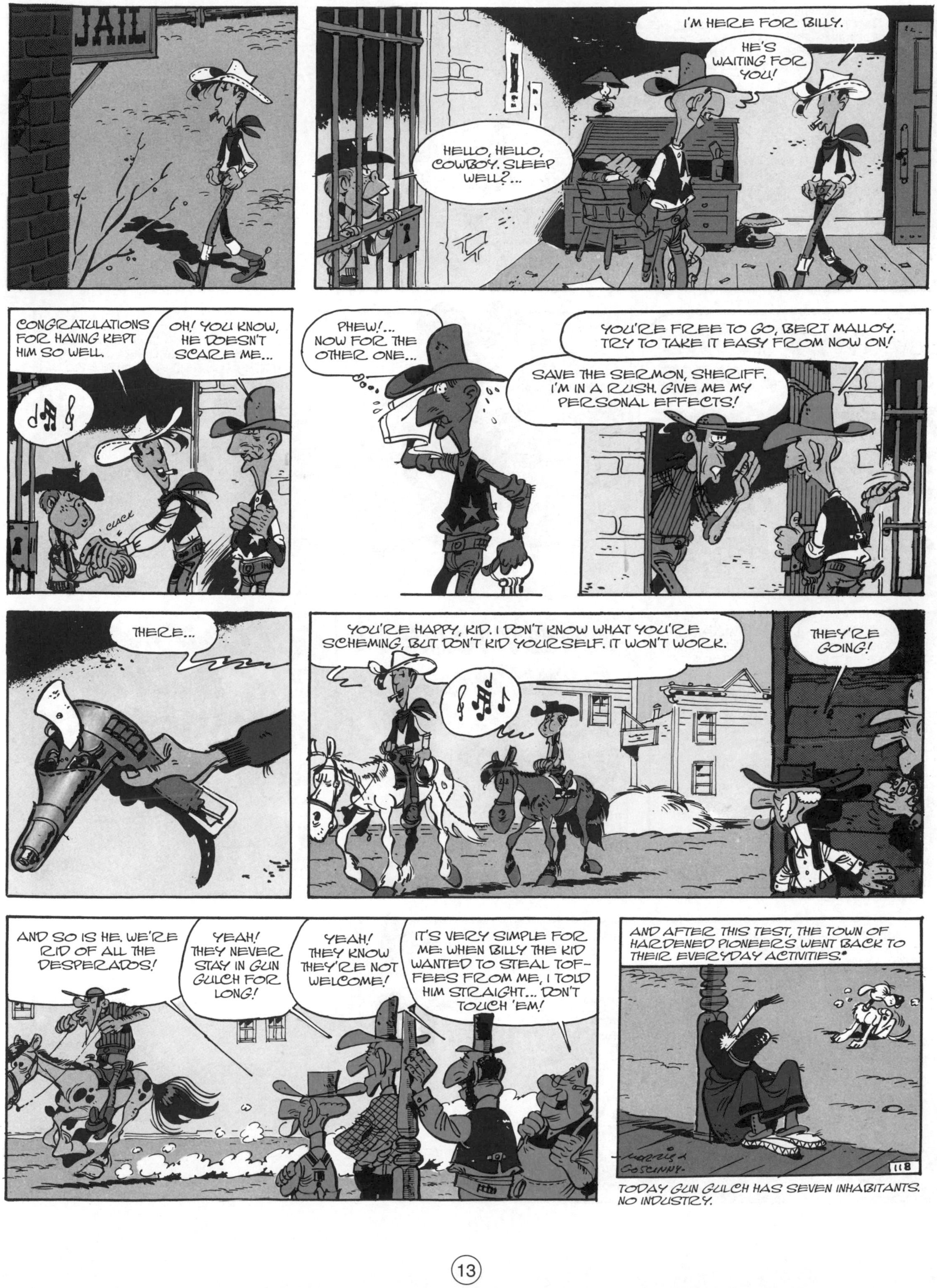
JAIL
I'M HERE FOR BILLY.
HE'S WAITING FOR YOU!
HELLO, HELLO, COWBOY. SLEEP WELL?...
CONGRATULATIONS FOR HAVING KEPT HIM SO WELL.
OH! YOU KNOW, HE DOESN'T SCARE ME...
CLACK
PHEW!... NOW FOR THE OTHER ONE...
YOU'RE FREE TO GO, BERT MALLOY. TRY TO TAKE IT EASY FROM NOW ON!
SAVE THE SERMON, SHERIFF. I'M IN A RUSH. GIVE ME MY PERSONAL EFFECTS!
THERE...
YOU'RE HAPPY, KID. I DON'T KNOW WHAT YOU'RE SCHEMING, BUT DON'T KID YOURSELF. IT WON'T WORK.
THEY'RE GOING!
AND SO IS HE. WE'RE RID OF ALL THE DESPERADOS!
YEAH! THEY NEVER STAY IN GUN GULCH FOR LONG!
YEAH! THEY KNOW THEY'RE NOT WELCOME!
IT'S VERY SIMPLE FOR ME: WHEN BILLY THE KID WANTED TO STEAL TOFFEES FROM ME, I TOLD HIM STRAIGHT... DON'T TOUCH 'EM!
AND AFTER THIS TEST, THE TOWN OF HARDENED PIONEERS WENT BACK TO THEIR EVERYDAY ACTIVITIES.*
MORRIS & GOSCINNY
118

TODAY GUN GULCH HAS SEVEN INHABITANTS. NO INDUSTRY.

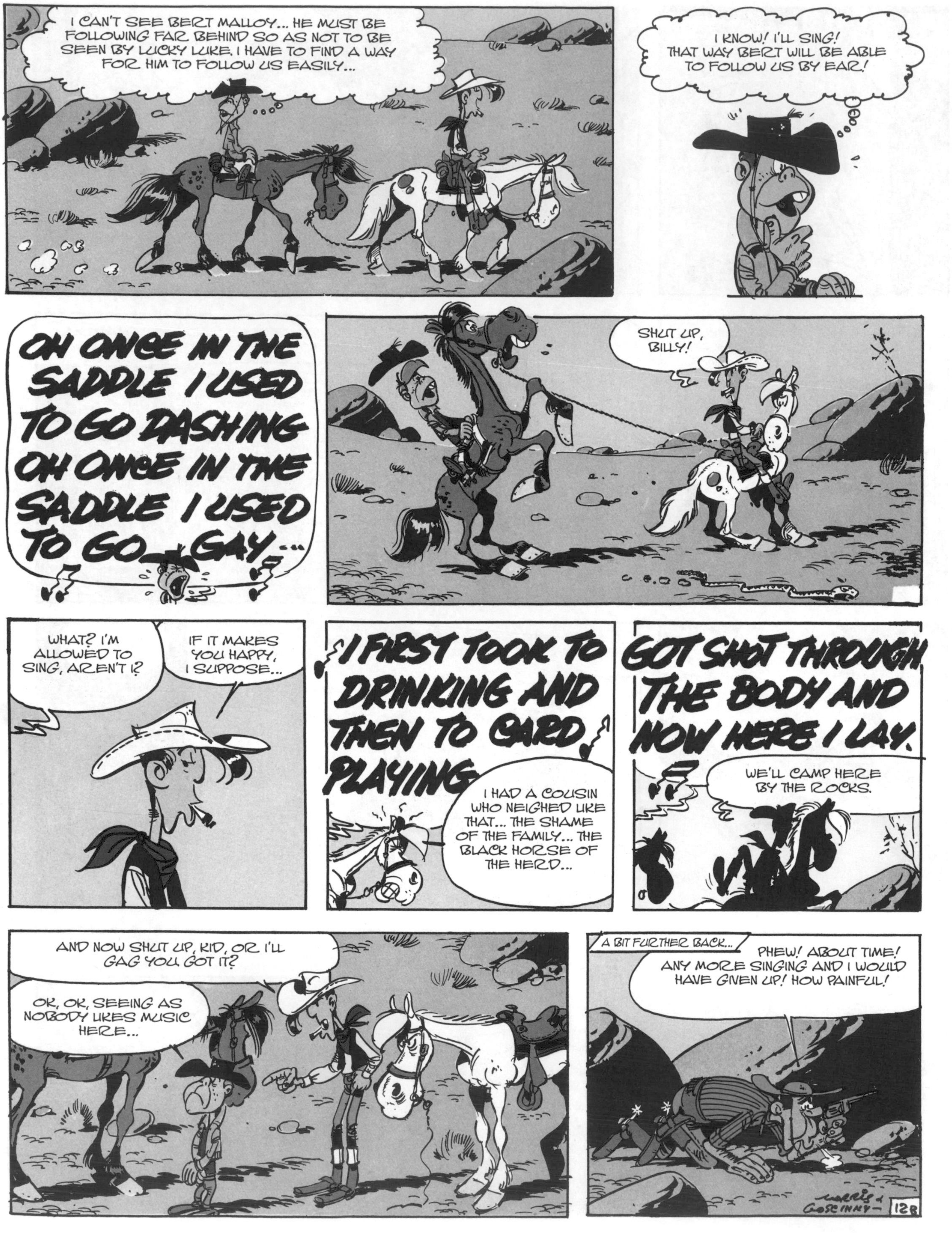
I CAN'T SEE BERT MALLOY... HE MUST BE FOLLOWING FAR BEHIND SO AS NOT TO BE SEEN BY LUCKY LUKE. I HAVE TO FIND A WAY FOR HIM TO FOLLOW US EASILY...
I KNOW! I'LL SING! THAT WAY BERT WILL BE ABLE TO FOLLOW US BY EAR!
OH ONCE IN THE SADDLE I USED TO GO DASHING OH ONCE IN THE SADDLE I USED TO GO GAY...
SHUT UP, BILLY!
WHAT? I'M ALLOWED TO SING, AREN'T I?
IF IT MAKES YOU HAPPY, I SUPPOSE...
I FIRST TOOK TO DRINKING AND THEN TO CARD PLAYING
I HAD A COUSIN WHO NEIGHED LIKE THAT... THE SHAME OF THE FAMILY... THE BLACK HORSE OF THE HERD...
GOT SHOT THROUGH THE BODY AND NOW HERE I LAY.
WE'LL CAMP HERE BY THE ROCKS.
AND NOW SHUT UP, KID, OR I'LL GAG YOU GOT IT?
OK, OK, SEEING AS NOBODY LIKES MUSIC HERE...
A BIT FURTHER BACK...
PHEW! ABOUT TIME! ANY MORE SINGING AND I WOULD HAVE GIVEN UP! HOW PAINFUL!
MORRIS & GOSCINNY
12B

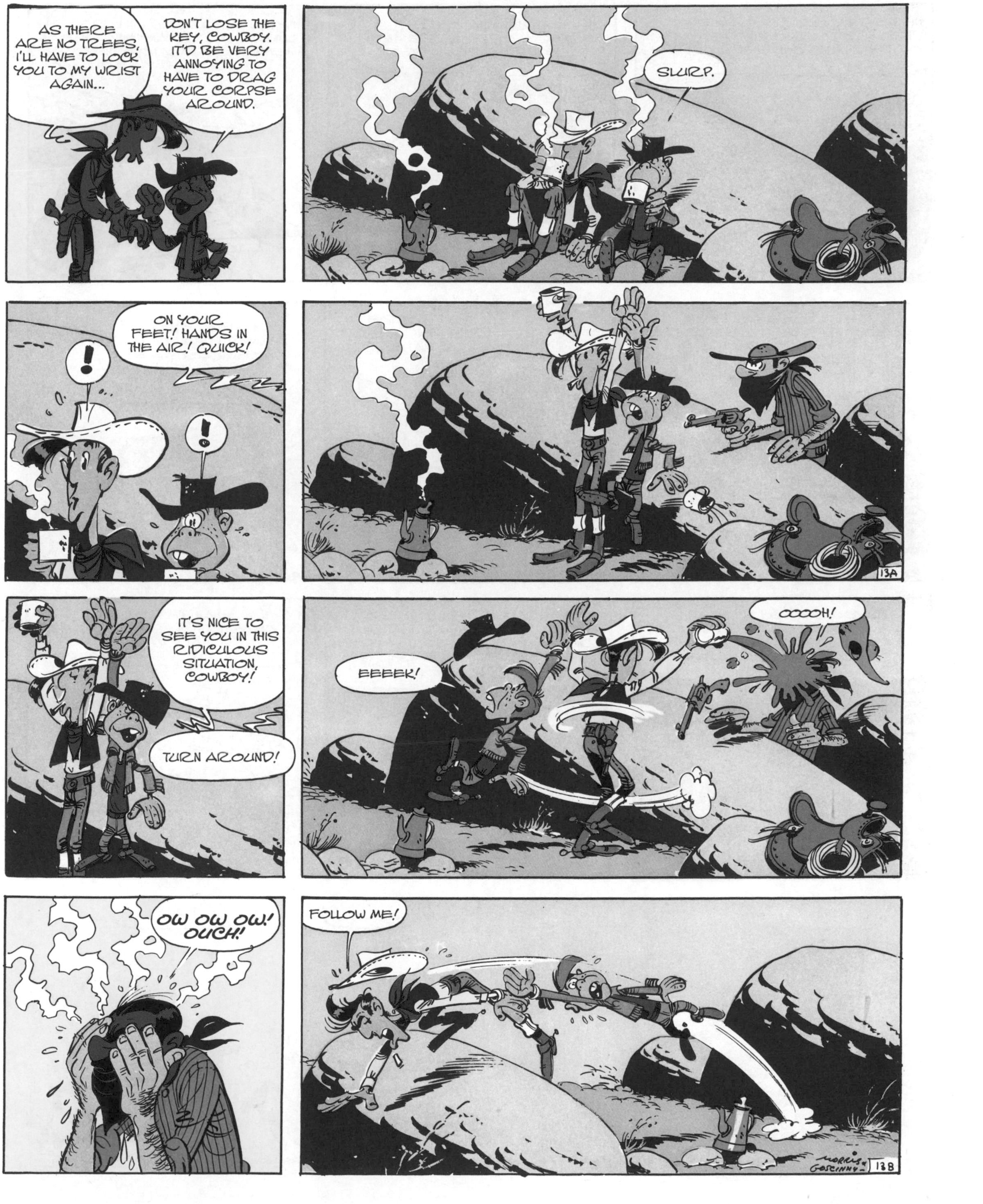

AS THERE ARE NO TREES, I'LL HAVE TO LOCK YOU TO MY WRIST AGAIN...
DON'T LOSE THE KEY, COWBOY. IT'D BE VERY ANNOYING TO HAVE TO DRAG YOUR CORPSE AROUND.
SLURP.
!
!
ON YOUR FEET! HANDS IN THE AIR! QUICK!
13A
IT'S NICE TO SEE YOU IN THIS RIDICULOUS SITUATION, COWBOY!
TURN AROUND!
EEEEK!
OOOOH!
OW OW OW! OUCH!
FOLLOW ME!
MORRIS GOSCINNY
13B

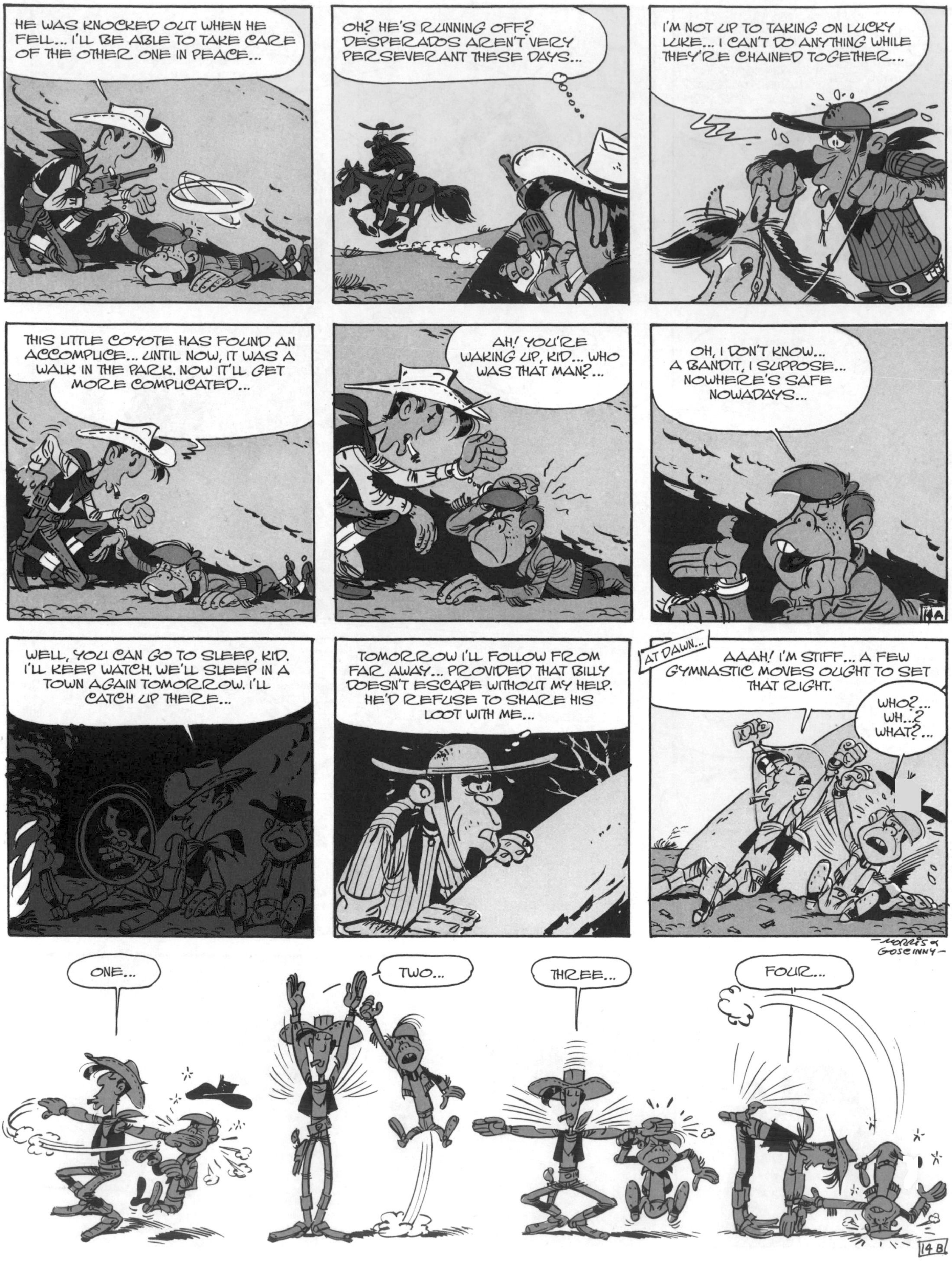
HE WAS KNOCKED OUT WHEN HE FELL... I'LL BE ABLE TO TAKE CARE OF THE OTHER ONE IN PEACE...
OH? HE'S RUNNING OFF? DESPERADOS AREN'T VERY PERSEVERANT THESE DAYS...
I'M NOT UP TO TAKING ON LUCKY LUKE... I CAN'T DO ANYTHING WHILE THEY'RE CHAINED TOGETHER...
THIS LITTLE COYOTE HAS FOUND AN ACCOMPLICE... UNTIL NOW, IT WAS A WALK IN THE PARK. NOW IT'LL GET MORE COMPLICATED...
AH! YOU'RE WAKING UP, KID... WHO WAS THAT MAN?...
OH, I DON'T KNOW... A BANDIT, I SUPPOSE... NOWHERE'S SAFE NOWADAYS...
14A
WELL, YOU CAN GO TO SLEEP, KID. I'LL KEEP WATCH. WE'LL SLEEP IN A TOWN AGAIN TOMORROW. I'LL CATCH UP THERE...
TOMORROW I'LL FOLLOW FROM FAR AWAY... PROVIDED THAT BILLY DOESN'T ESCAPE WITHOUT MY HELP. HE'D REFUSE TO SHARE HIS LOOT WITH ME...
AT DAWN...
AAAH! I'M STIFF... A FEW GYMNASTIC MOVES OUGHT TO SET THAT RIGHT.
WHO?... WH...? WHAT?...
MORRIS & GOSCINNY
ONE...
TWO...
THREE...
FOUR...
14B

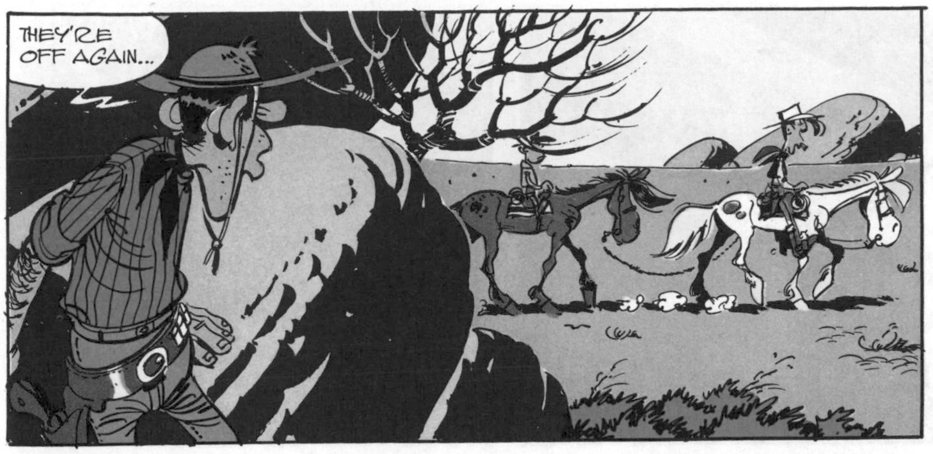
THEY'RE OFF AGAIN...

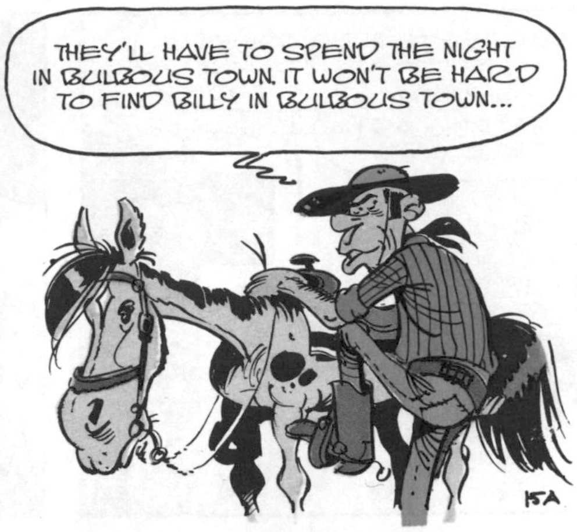
THEY'LL HAVE TO SPEND THE NIGHT IN BULBOUS TOWN. IT WON'T BE HARD TO FIND BILLY IN BULBOUS TOWN...

INDEED, BULBOUS TOWN WAS PROUDLY THE LITTLEST TOWN WITH THE BIGGEST FUTURE. AN OLD STAGECOACH STOP, IT CONSISTED...

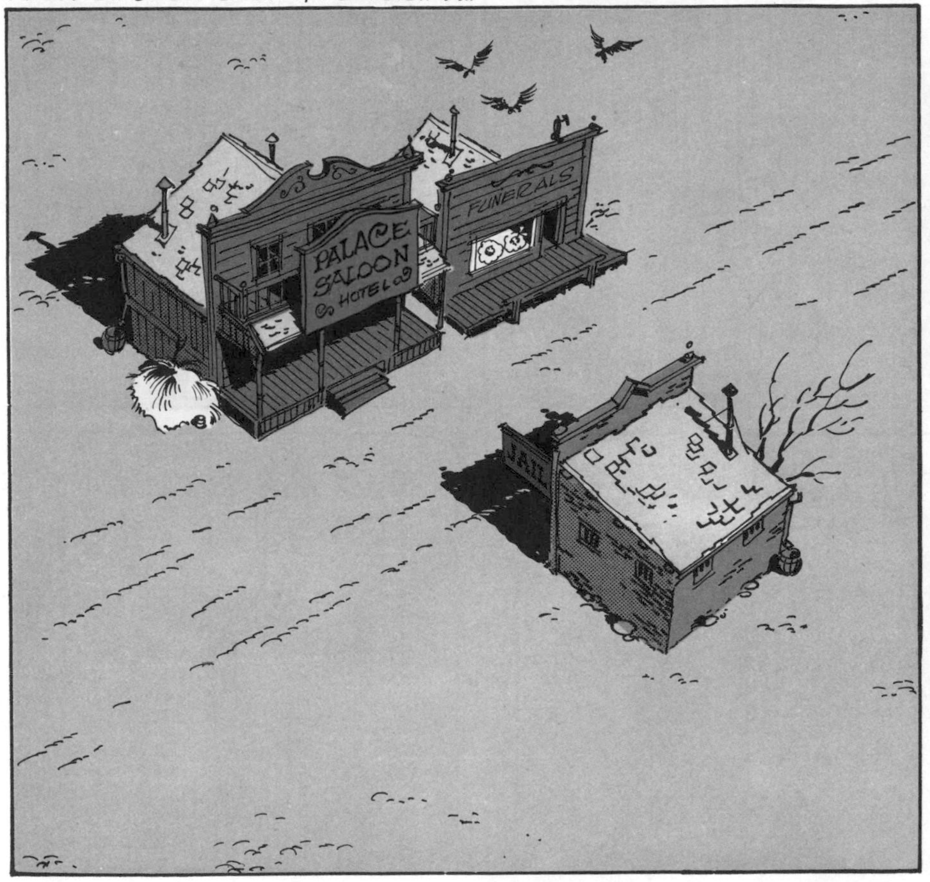
PALACE SALOON HOTEL
FUNERALS
JAIL

...MOSTLY OF A HOTEL WITH A SALOON, WHERE PEOPLE WHO LEFT JAIL WENT TO CELEBRATE THEIR FREEDOM...

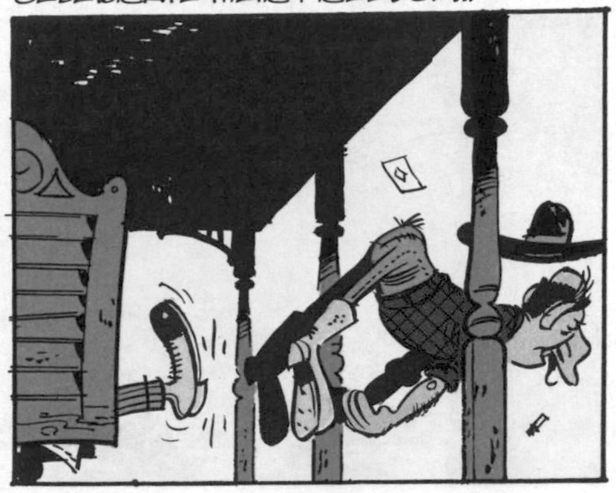

...A JAIL, WHICH WAS THERE FOR THOSE WHO CELEBRATED THEIR FREEDOM TOO MUCH...

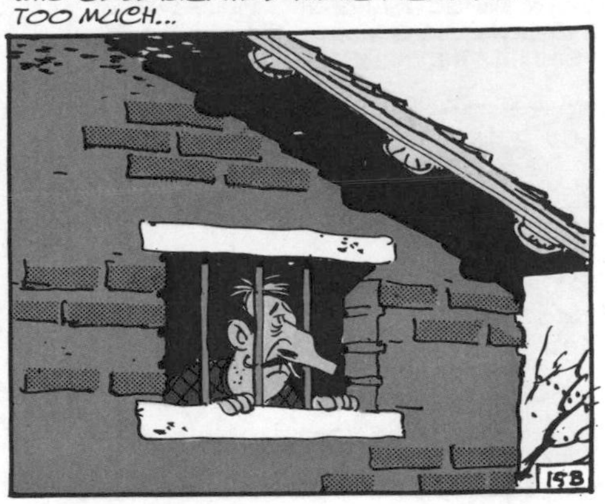

...AND AN UNDERTAKER, WHO WAS THERE TO LOOK AFTER THOSE WHO HAD ACCIDENTS CROSSING OVER FROM THE SALOON TO THE JAIL OR VICE VERSA.

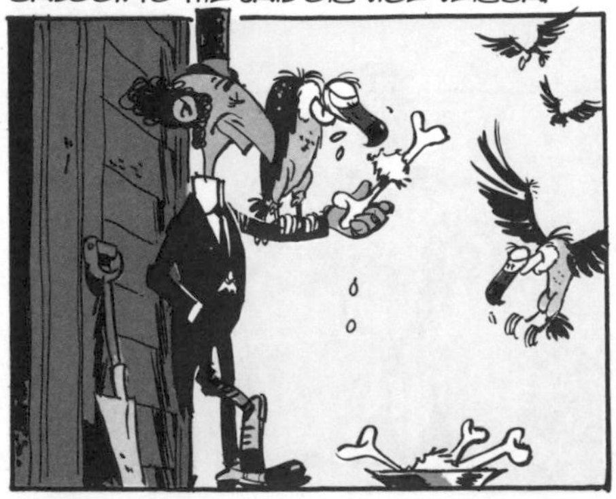

LET US NOT FORGET THAT THE MAYOR IS THE OWNER OF THE HOTEL AND SALOON, THAT THE SHERIFF IS HIS COUSIN AND THAT THE UNDERTAKER IS THE BROTHER-IN-LAW OF THE MAYOR'S COUSIN(*).

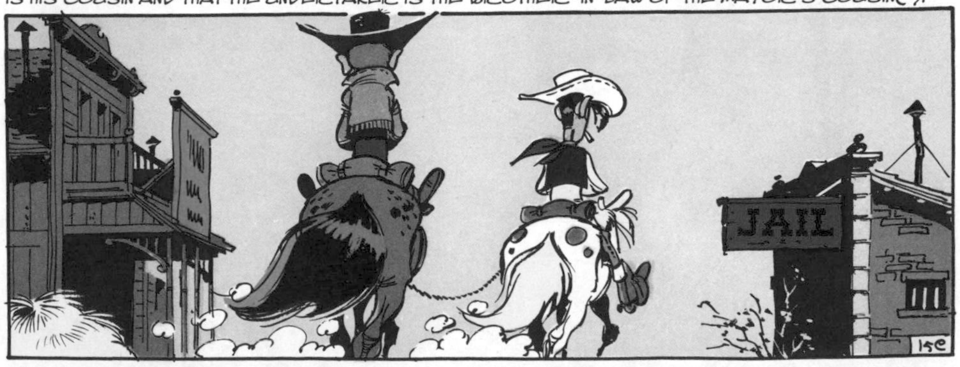
JAIL

(*) TODAY, BULBOUS TOWN IS A CITY OF 318,765 INHABITANTS, WITH 3857 SALOONS, 4,230 FUNERAL HOMES AND THE MOST MODERN JAIL IN THE USA.

I'M PUTTING YOU IN THE JAIL, KID...

ANYWHERE YOU LIKE, AS LONG AS I'M ALONE, COWBOY!

FOR THE SHERIFF, SEE THE SALOON OPPOSITE.

HOWDY...

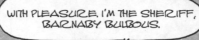

I'M MATHIAS BULBOUS, THE MAYOR OF BULBOUS TOWN. WE'RE CELEBRATING THE 10TH ANNIVERSARY OF THE SALOON, THE JAIL AND THE FUNERAL HOME. WE'RE PRETTY MUCH CELEBRATING THE 10TH ANNIVERSARY OF OUR BELOVED CITY!

NICE TO MEET YOU... I'M LUCKY LUKE AND I'M ESCORTING THIS PRISONER TO BRONCO PUEBLO. I'D LIKE HIM TO SPEND THE NIGHT IN YOUR JAIL.

WITH PLEASURE. I'M THE SHERIFF, BARNABY BULBOUS.

AND I'M BILLY THE KID!

BE ON YOUR WAY!

NO! I'VE HAD ENOUGH OF FINDING CHICKENS ON MY JOURNEY! IF YOU WANT TO STAY LIVE CHICKENS, WE'RE STAYING HERE!

AND IF NOT, I'D LIKE YOU TO KNOW THAT I'M NEFARIOUS GRAVE, FUNERALS DAY AND NIGHT, AT YOUR SERVICE.

MORRIS & GOSCINNY

16B

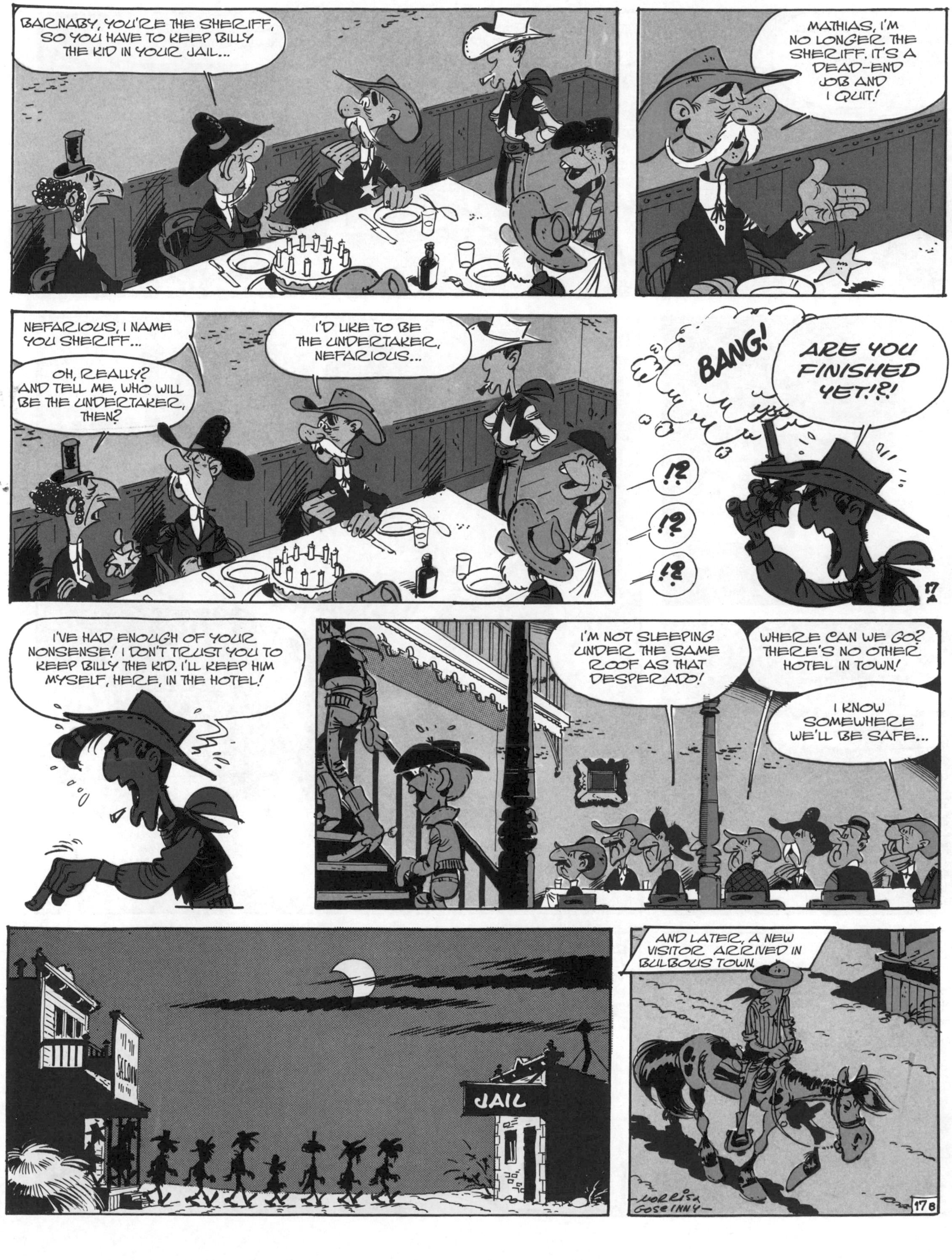

BARNABY, YOU'RE THE SHERIFF, SO YOU HAVE TO KEEP BILLY THE KID IN YOUR JAIL...
MATHIAS, I'M NO LONGER THE SHERIFF. IT'S A DEAD-END JOB AND I QUIT!
NEFARIOUS, I NAME YOU SHERIFF...
OH, REALLY? AND TELL ME, WHO WILL BE THE UNDERTAKER, THEN?
I'D LIKE TO BE THE UNDERTAKER, NEFARIOUS...
BANG!
ARE YOU FINISHED YET!?!
!?
!?
!?
I'VE HAD ENOUGH OF YOUR NONSENSE! I DON'T TRUST YOU TO KEEP BILLY THE KID. I'LL KEEP HIM MYSELF, HERE, IN THE HOTEL!
I'M NOT SLEEPING UNDER THE SAME ROOF AS THAT DESPERADO!
WHERE CAN WE GO? THERE'S NO OTHER HOTEL IN TOWN!
I KNOW SOMEWHERE WE'LL BE SAFE...
SALOON
JAIL
AND LATER, A NEW VISITOR ARRIVED IN BULBOUS TOWN.
MORRIS GOSCINNY

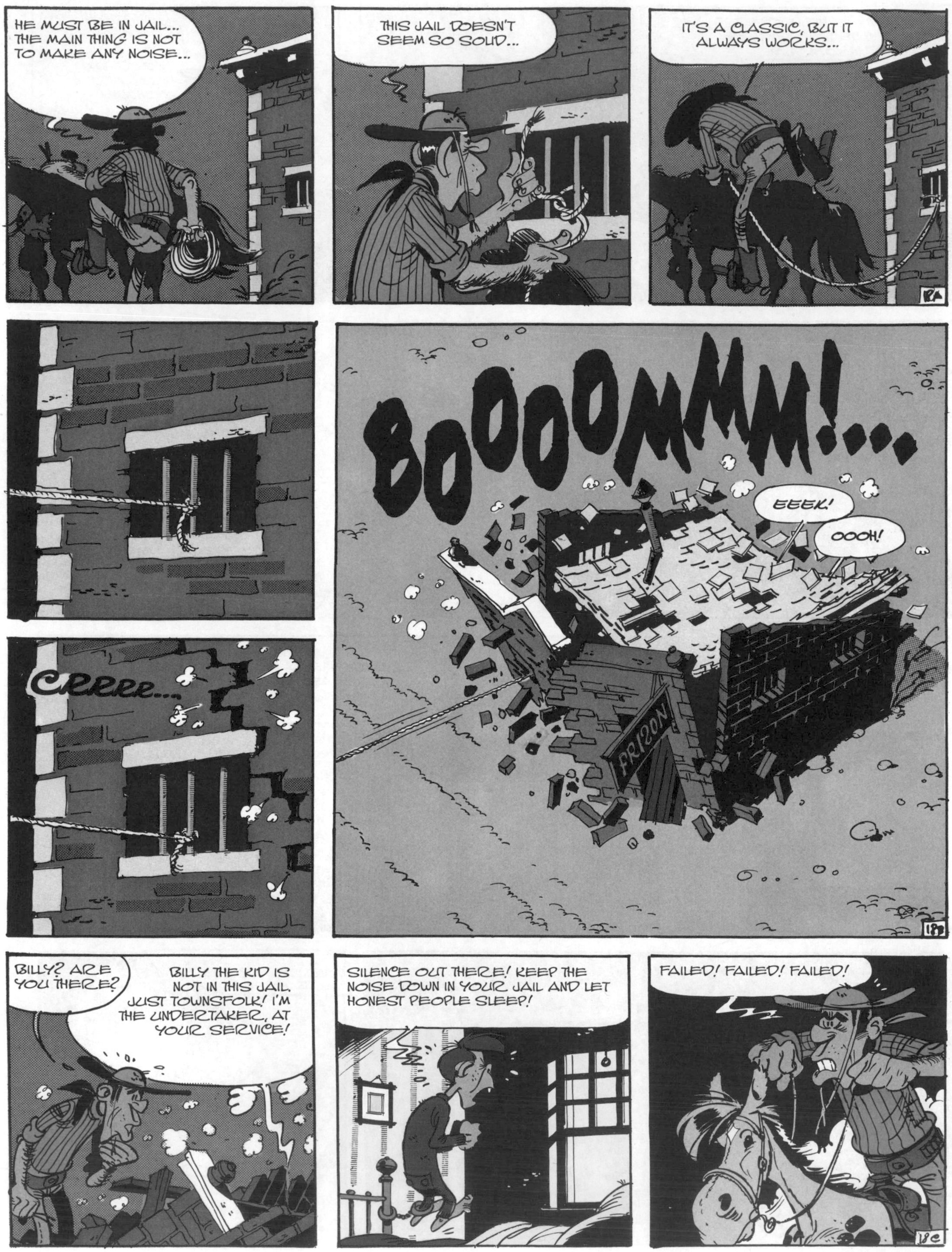
HE MUST BE IN JAIL... THE MAIN THING IS NOT TO MAKE ANY NOISE...
THIS JAIL DOESN'T SEEM SO SOLID...
IT'S A CLASSIC, BUT IT ALWAYS WORKS...
CRRRR...
BOOOOMMM!...
EEEK!
OOOH!
PRISON
BILLY? ARE YOU THERE?
BILLY THE KID IS NOT IN THIS JAIL. JUST TOWNSFOLK! I'M THE UNDERTAKER, AT YOUR SERVICE!
SILENCE OUT THERE! KEEP THE NOISE DOWN IN YOUR JAIL AND LET HONEST PEOPLE SLEEP!
FAILED! FAILED! FAILED!

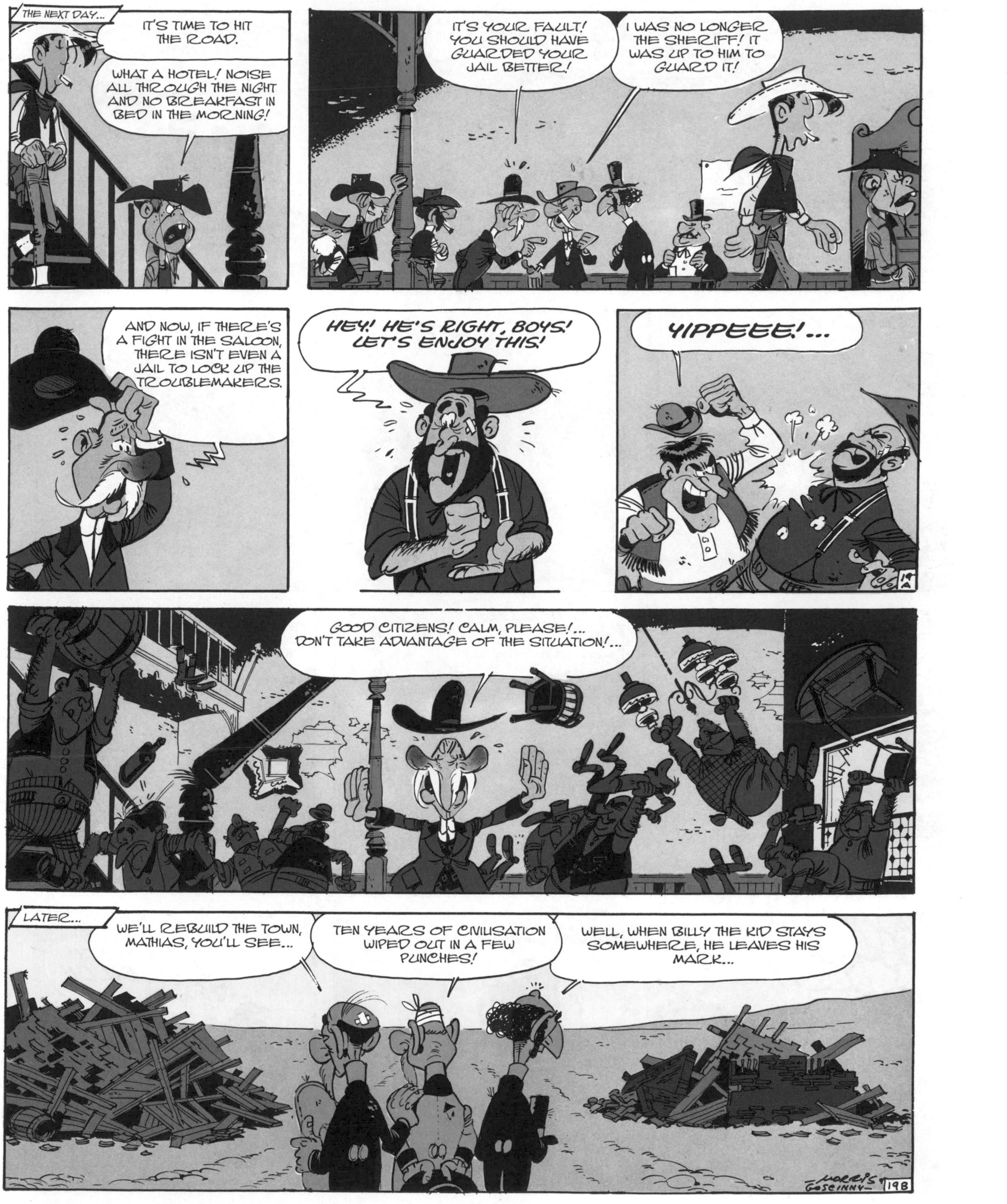
THE NEXT DAY...
IT'S TIME TO HIT THE ROAD.
WHAT A HOTEL! NOISE ALL THROUGH THE NIGHT AND NO BREAKFAST IN BED IN THE MORNING!
IT'S YOUR FAULT! YOU SHOULD HAVE GUARDED YOUR JAIL BETTER!
I WAS NO LONGER THE SHERIFF! IT WAS UP TO HIM TO GUARD IT!
AND NOW, IF THERE'S A FIGHT IN THE SALOON, THERE ISN'T EVEN A JAIL TO LOCK UP THE TROUBLEMAKERS.
HEY! HE'S RIGHT, BOYS! LET'S ENJOY THIS!
YIPPEEE!...
GOOD CITIZENS! CALM, PLEASE!... DON'T TAKE ADVANTAGE OF THE SITUATION!...
LATER...
WE'LL REBUILD THE TOWN, MATHIAS, YOU'LL SEE...
TEN YEARS OF CIVILISATION WIPED OUT IN A FEW PUNCHES!
WELL, WHEN BILLY THE KID STAYS SOMEWHERE, HE LEAVES HIS MARK...
MORRIS GOSCINNY
19B

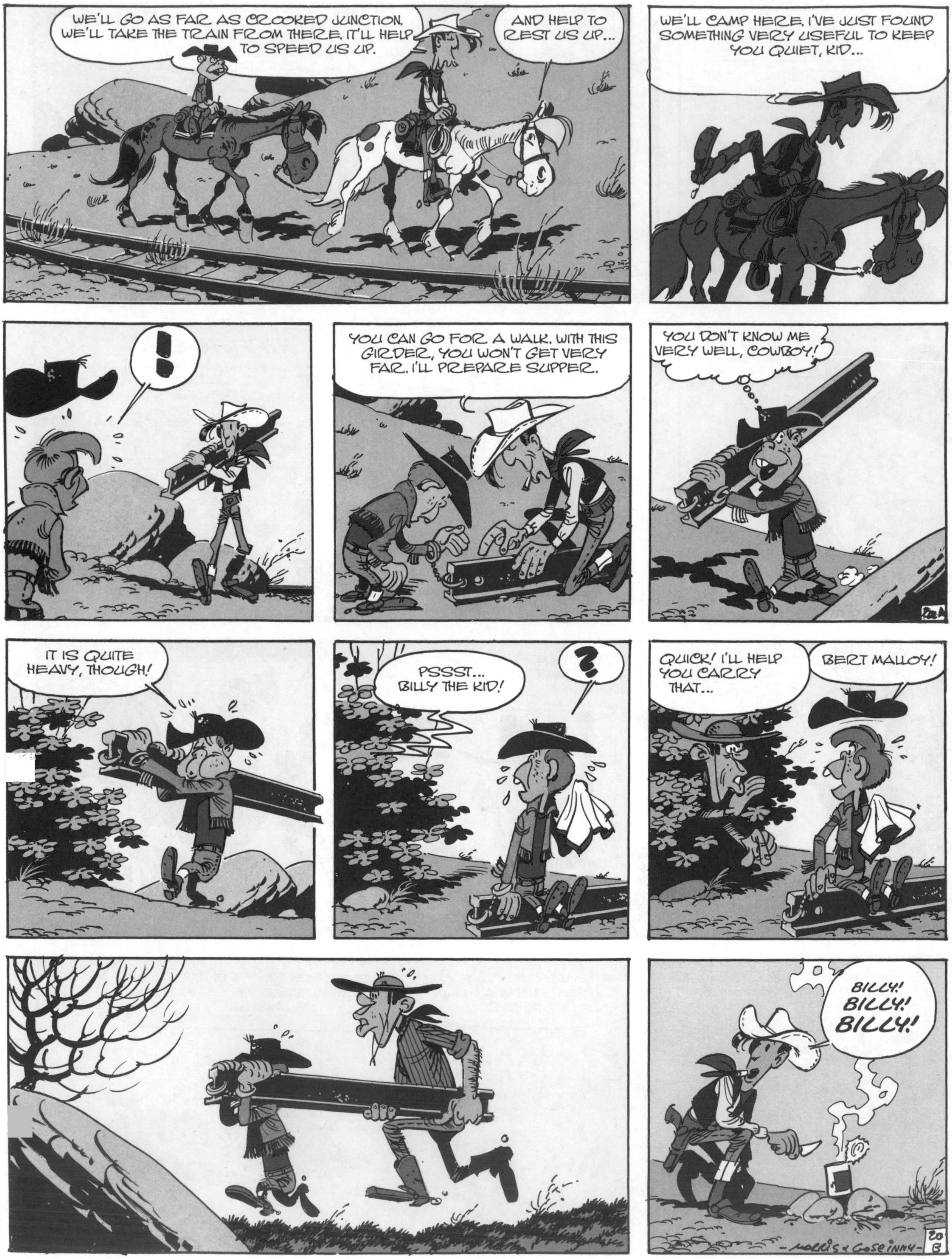
WE'LL GO AS FAR AS CROOKED JUNCTION. WE'LL TAKE THE TRAIN FROM THERE. IT'LL HELP TO SPEED US UP.
AND HELP TO REST US UP...
WE'LL CAMP HERE. I'VE JUST FOUND SOMETHING VERY USEFUL TO KEEP YOU QUIET, KID...
!
YOU CAN GO FOR A WALK. WITH THIS GIRDER, YOU WON'T GET VERY FAR. I'LL PREPARE SUPPER.
YOU DON'T KNOW ME VERY WELL, COWBOY!
IT IS QUITE HEAVY, THOUGH!
PSSST... BILLY THE KID!
?
QUICK! I'LL HELP YOU CARRY THAT...
BERT MALLOY!
BILLY! BILLY! BILLY!
MORRIS & GOSCINNY

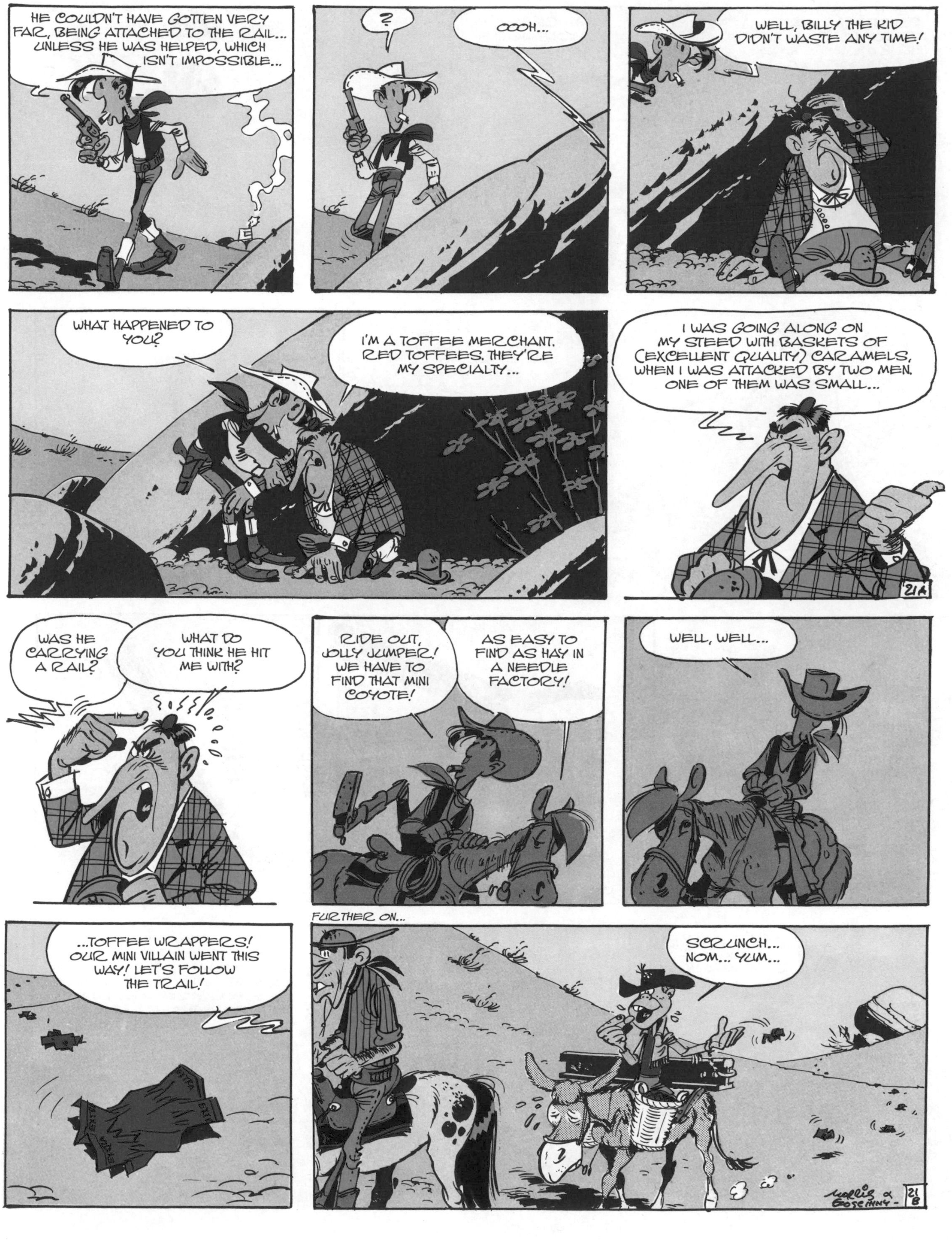

HE COULDN'T HAVE GOTTEN VERY FAR, BEING ATTACHED TO THE RAIL... UNLESS HE WAS HELPED, WHICH ISN'T IMPOSSIBLE...
?
OOOH...
WELL, BILLY THE KID DIDN'T WASTE ANY TIME!
WHAT HAPPENED TO YOU?
I'M A TOFFEE MERCHANT. RED TOFFEES. THEY'RE MY SPECIALTY...
I WAS GOING ALONG ON MY STEED WITH BASKETS OF (EXCELLENT QUALITY) CARAMELS, WHEN I WAS ATTACKED BY TWO MEN. ONE OF THEM WAS SMALL...
21A
WAS HE CARRYING A RAIL?
WHAT DO YOU THINK HE HIT ME WITH?
RIDE OUT, JOLLY JUMPER! WE HAVE TO FIND THAT MINI COYOTE!
AS EASY TO FIND AS HAY IN A NEEDLE FACTORY!
WELL, WELL...
...TOFFEE WRAPPERS! OUR MINI VILLAIN WENT THIS WAY! LET'S FOLLOW THE TRAIL!
FURTHER ON...
SCRUNCH... NOM... YUM...
MORRIS & GOSCINNY
21B

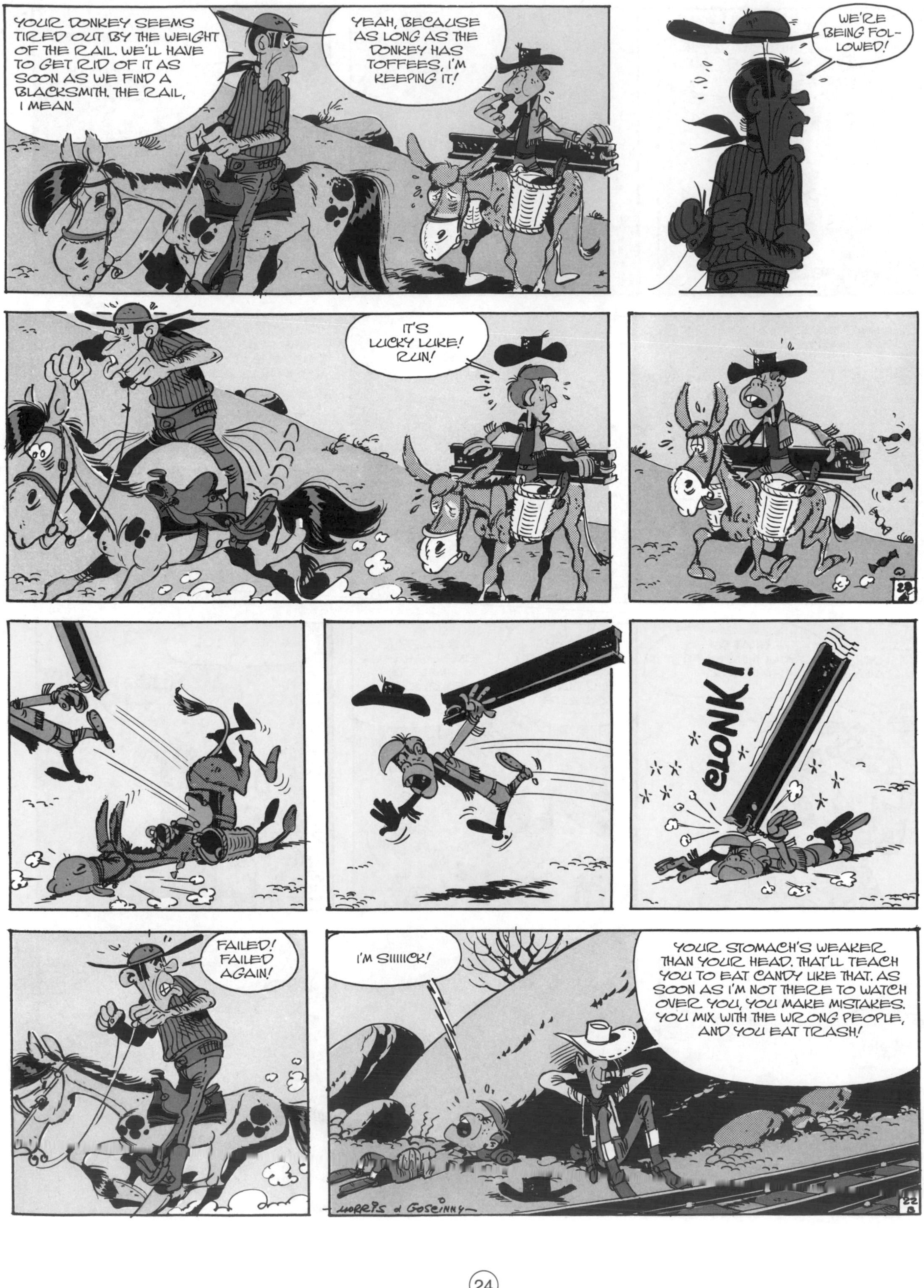
YOUR DONKEY SEEMS TIRED OUT BY THE WEIGHT OF THE RAIL. WE'LL HAVE TO GET RID OF IT AS SOON AS WE FIND A BLACKSMITH. THE RAIL, I MEAN.
YEAH, BECAUSE AS LONG AS THE DONKEY HAS TOFFEES, I'M KEEPING IT!
WE'RE BEING FOL-LOWED!
IT'S LUCKY LUKE! RUN!
CLONK!
FAILED! FAILED AGAIN!
I'M SIIIIICK!
YOUR STOMACH'S WEAKER THAN YOUR HEAD. THAT'LL TEACH YOU TO EAT CANDY LIKE THAT. AS SOON AS I'M NOT THERE TO WATCH OVER YOU, YOU MAKE MISTAKES. YOU MIX WITH THE WRONG PEOPLE, AND YOU EAT TRASH!
MORRIS & GOSCINNY

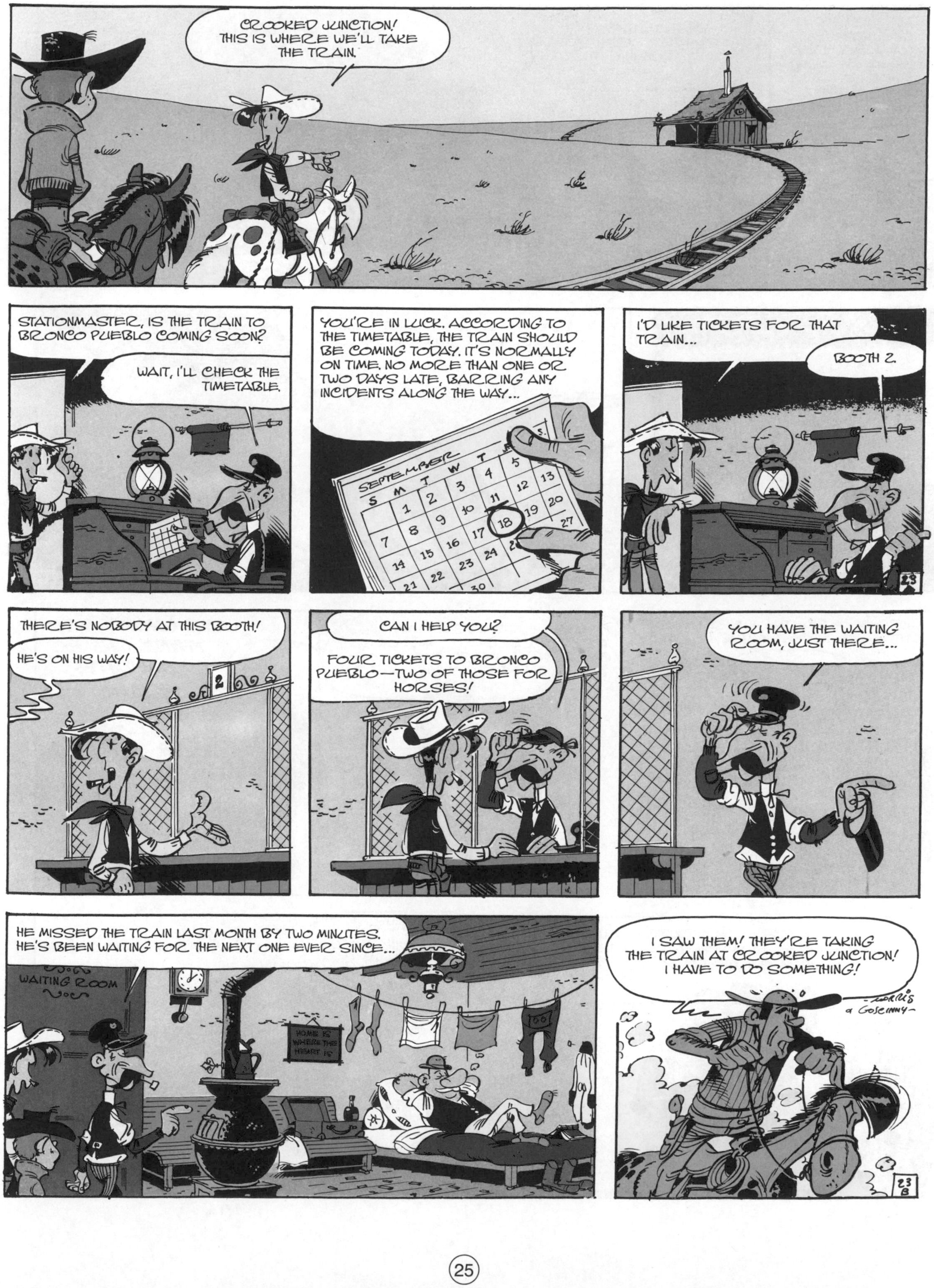

CROOKED JUNCTION! THIS IS WHERE WE'LL TAKE THE TRAIN.
STATIONMASTER, IS THE TRAIN TO BRONCO PUEBLO COMING SOON?
WAIT, I'LL CHECK THE TIMETABLE.
YOU'RE IN LUCK. ACCORDING TO THE TIMETABLE, THE TRAIN SHOULD BE COMING TODAY. IT'S NORMALLY ON TIME. NO MORE THAN ONE OR TWO DAYS LATE, BARRING ANY INCIDENTS ALONG THE WAY...
SEPTEMBER
I'D LIKE TICKETS FOR THAT TRAIN...
BOOTH 2.
THERE'S NOBODY AT THIS BOOTH!
HE'S ON HIS WAY!
CAN I HELP YOU?
FOUR TICKETS TO BRONCO PUEBLO—TWO OF THOSE FOR HORSES!
YOU HAVE THE WAITING ROOM, JUST THERE...
HE MISSED THE TRAIN LAST MONTH BY TWO MINUTES. HE'S BEEN WAITING FOR THE NEXT ONE EVER SINCE...
WAITING ROOM
HOME IS WHERE THE HEART IS
I SAW THEM! THEY'RE TAKING THE TRAIN AT CROOKED JUNCTION! I HAVE TO DO SOMETHING!

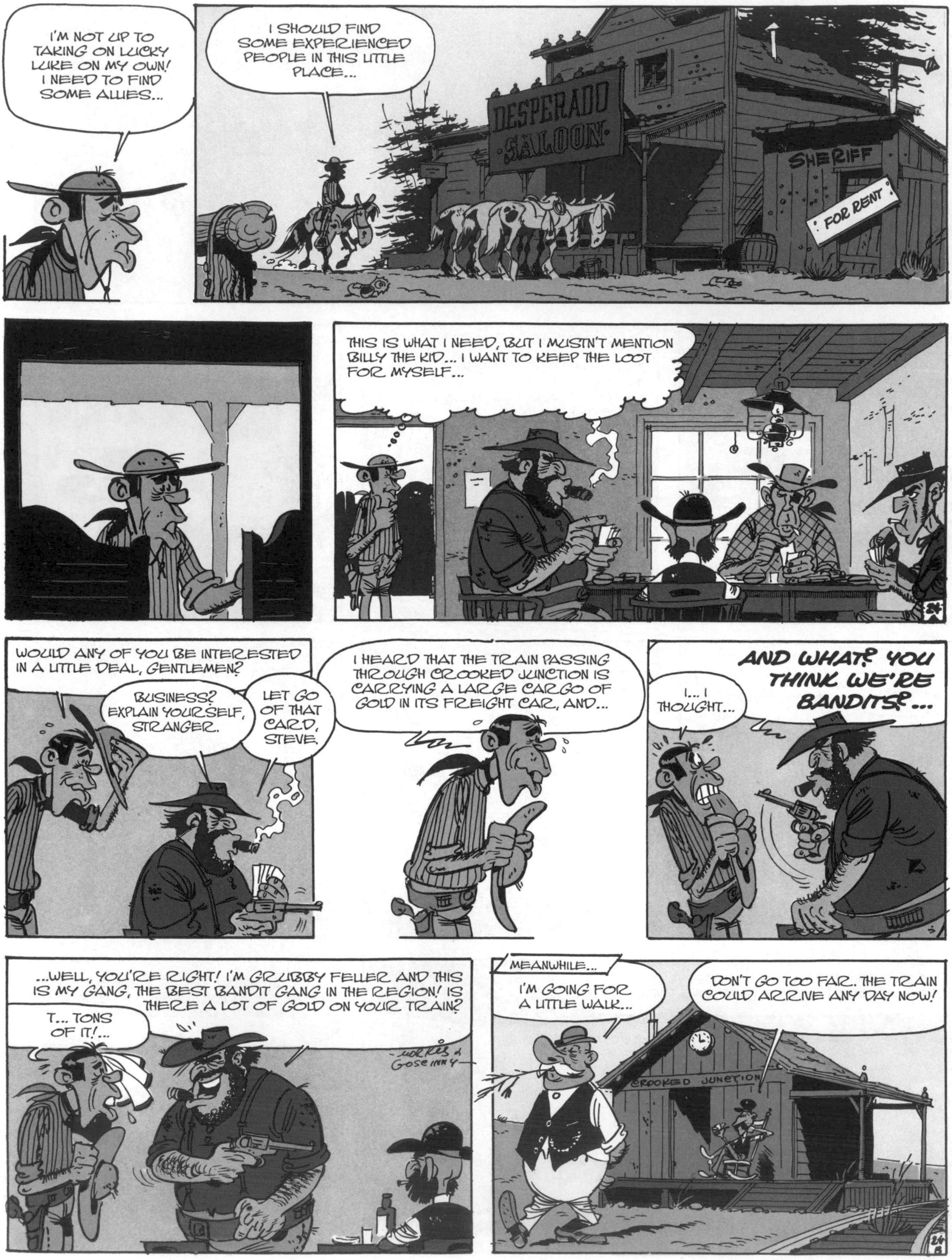

I'M NOT UP TO TAKING ON LUCKY LUKE ON MY OWN! I NEED TO FIND SOME ALLIES...
I SHOULD FIND SOME EXPERIENCED PEOPLE IN THIS LITTLE PLACE...
DESPERADO SALOON
SHERIFF
FOR RENT
THIS IS WHAT I NEED, BUT I MUSTN'T MENTION BILLY THE KID... I WANT TO KEEP THE LOOT FOR MYSELF...
WOULD ANY OF YOU BE INTERESTED IN A LITTLE DEAL, GENTLEMEN?
BUSINESS? EXPLAIN YOURSELF, STRANGER.
LET GO OF THAT CARD, STEVE.
I HEARD THAT THE TRAIN PASSING THROUGH CROOKED JUNCTION IS CARRYING A LARGE CARGO OF GOLD IN ITS FREIGHT CAR, AND...
I... I THOUGHT...
AND WHAT? YOU THINK WE'RE BANDITS?...
...WELL, YOU'RE RIGHT! I'M GRUBBY FELLER AND THIS IS MY GANG, THE BEST BANDIT GANG IN THE REGION! IS THERE A LOT OF GOLD ON YOUR TRAIN?
T... TONS OF IT!...
MORRIS & GOSCINNY
MEANWHILE...
I'M GOING FOR A LITTLE WALK...
DON'T GO TOO FAR. THE TRAIN COULD ARRIVE ANY DAY NOW!
CROOKED JUNCTION

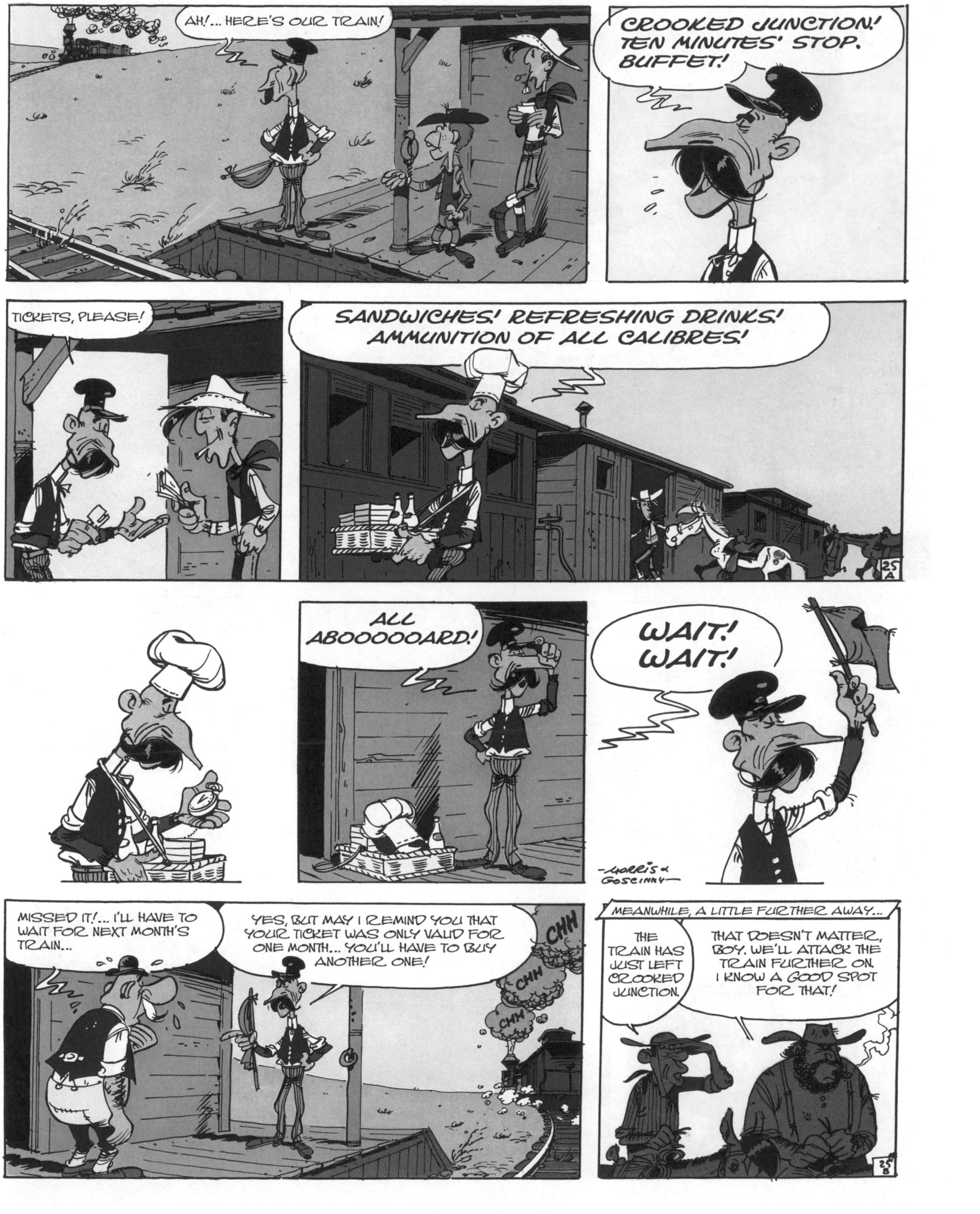
AH!... HERE'S OUR TRAIN!
CROOKED JUNCTION! TEN MINUTES' STOP. BUFFET!
TICKETS, PLEASE!
SANDWICHES! REFRESHING DRINKS! AMMUNITION OF ALL CALIBRES!
ALL ABOOOOOARD!
WAIT! WAIT!
MORRIS & GOSCINNY
MISSED IT!... I'LL HAVE TO WAIT FOR NEXT MONTH'S TRAIN...
YES, BUT MAY I REMIND YOU THAT YOUR TICKET WAS ONLY VALID FOR ONE MONTH... YOU'LL HAVE TO BUY ANOTHER ONE!
CHH
CHH
CHH
MEANWHILE, A LITTLE FURTHER AWAY...
THE TRAIN HAS JUST LEFT CROOKED JUNCTION.
THAT DOESN'T MATTER, BOY. WE'LL ATTACK THE TRAIN FURTHER ON. I KNOW A GOOD SPOT FOR THAT!

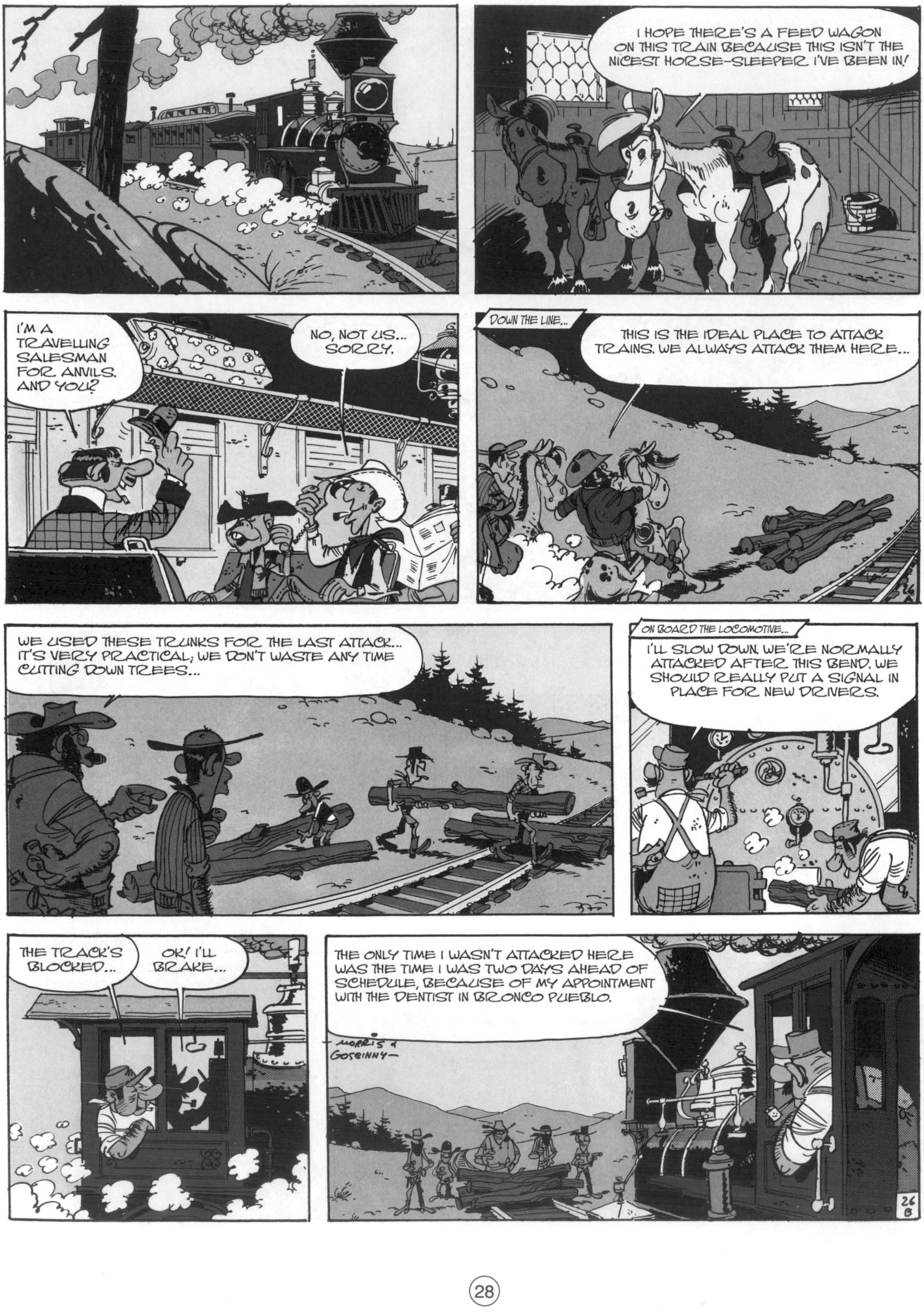
I HOPE THERE'S A FEED WAGON ON THIS TRAIN BECAUSE THIS ISN'T THE NICEST HORSE-SLEEPER I'VE BEEN IN!
I'M A TRAVELLING SALESMAN FOR ANVILS. AND YOU?
NO, NOT US... SORRY.
DOWN THE LINE...
THIS IS THE IDEAL PLACE TO ATTACK TRAINS. WE ALWAYS ATTACK THEM HERE...
WE USED THESE TRUNKS FOR THE LAST ATTACK... IT'S VERY PRACTICAL; WE DON'T WASTE ANY TIME CUTTING DOWN TREES...
ON BOARD THE LOCOMOTIVE...
I'LL SLOW DOWN. WE'RE NORMALLY ATTACKED AFTER THIS BEND. WE SHOULD REALLY PUT A SIGNAL IN PLACE FOR NEW DRIVERS.
THE TRACK'S BLOCKED...
OK! I'LL BRAKE...
THE ONLY TIME I WASN'T ATTACKED HERE WAS THE TIME I WAS TWO DAYS AHEAD OF SCHEDULE, BECAUSE OF MY APPOINTMENT WITH THE DENTIST IN BRONCO PUEBLO.
MORRIS & GOSCINNY
26 B

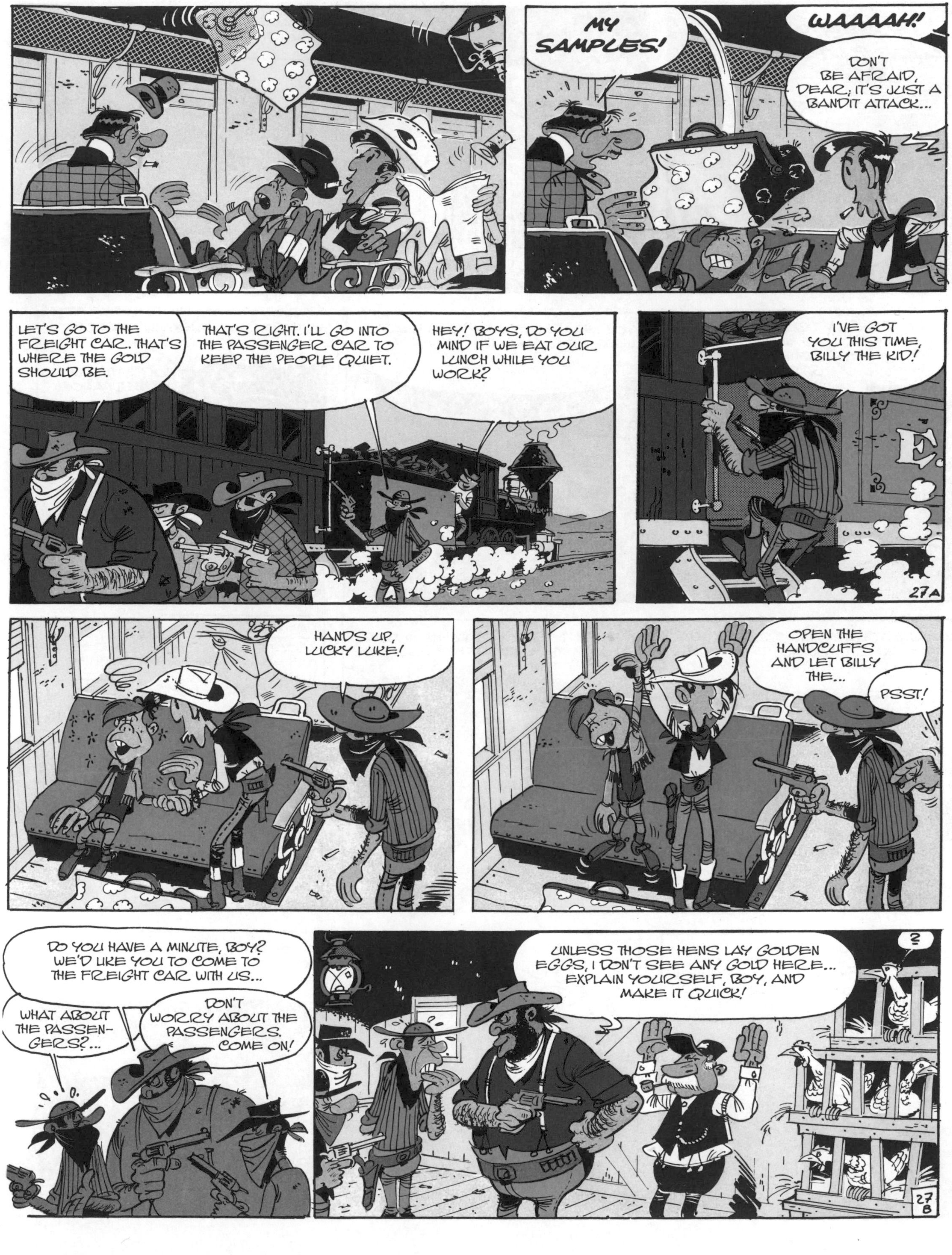

MY SAMPLES!
WAAAAH!
DON'T BE AFRAID, DEAR; IT'S JUST A BANDIT ATTACK...
LET'S GO TO THE FREIGHT CAR. THAT'S WHERE THE GOLD SHOULD BE.
THAT'S RIGHT. I'LL GO INTO THE PASSENGER CAR TO KEEP THE PEOPLE QUIET.
HEY! BOYS, DO YOU MIND IF WE EAT OUR LUNCH WHILE YOU WORK?
I'VE GOT YOU THIS TIME, BILLY THE KID!
27A
HANDS UP, LUCKY LUKE!
OPEN THE HANDCUFFS AND LET BILLY THE...
PSST!
DO YOU HAVE A MINUTE, BOY? WE'D LIKE YOU TO COME TO THE FREIGHT CAR WITH US...
WHAT ABOUT THE PASSEN-GERS?...
DON'T WORRY ABOUT THE PASSENGERS. COME ON!
UNLESS THOSE HENS LAY GOLDEN EGGS, I DON'T SEE ANY GOLD HERE... EXPLAIN YOURSELF, BOY, AND MAKE IT QUICK!
?
27 B

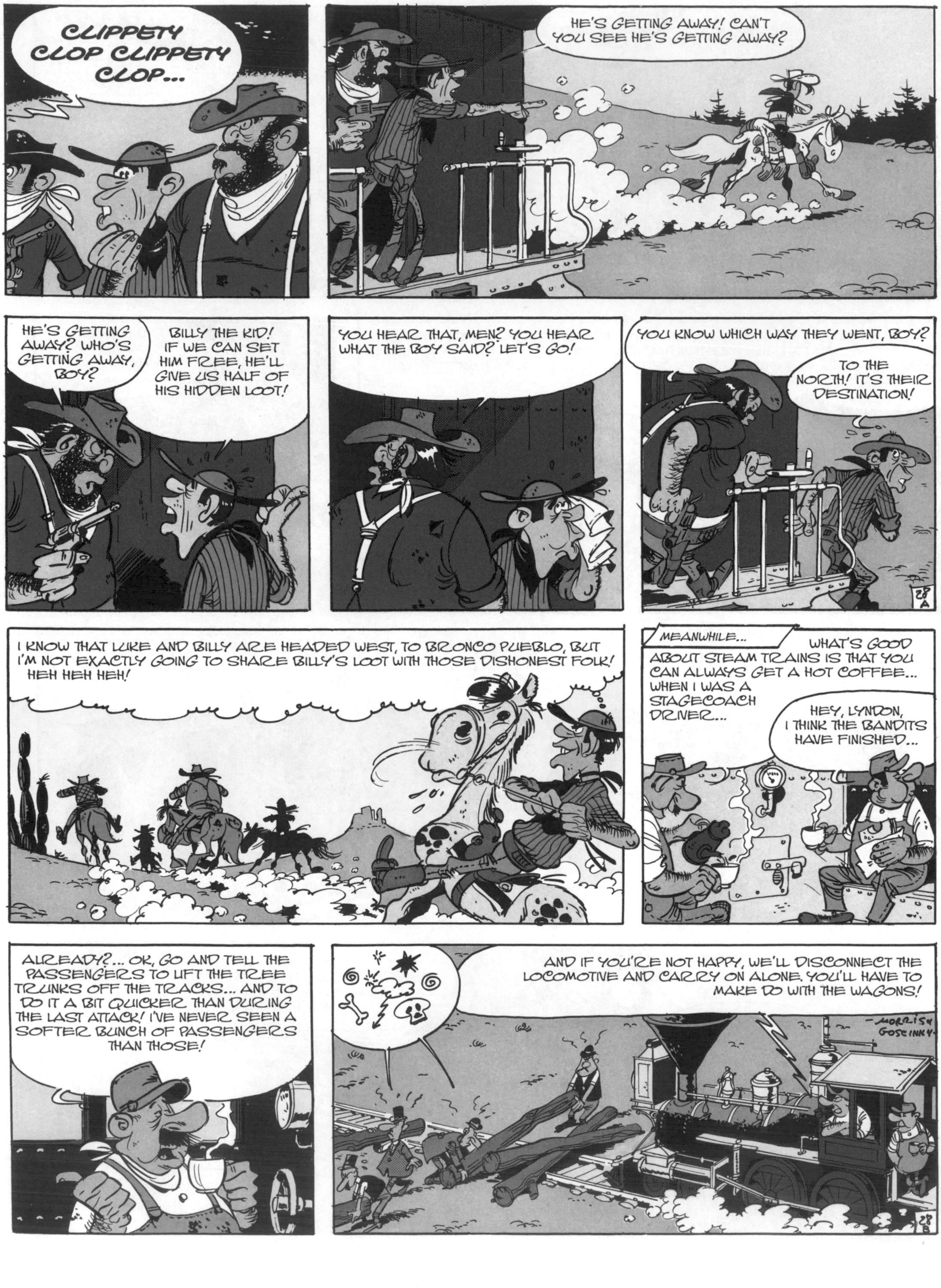
CLIPPETY CLOP CLIPPETY CLOP...
HE'S GETTING AWAY! CAN'T YOU SEE HE'S GETTING AWAY?
HE'S GETTING AWAY? WHO'S GETTING AWAY, BOY?
BILLY THE KID! IF WE CAN SET HIM FREE, HE'LL GIVE US HALF OF HIS HIDDEN LOOT!
YOU HEAR THAT, MEN? YOU HEAR WHAT THE BOY SAID? LET'S GO!
YOU KNOW WHICH WAY THEY WENT, BOY?
TO THE NORTH! IT'S THEIR DESTINATION!
I KNOW THAT LUKE AND BILLY ARE HEADED WEST, TO BRONCO PUEBLO, BUT I'M NOT EXACTLY GOING TO SHARE BILLY'S LOOT WITH THOSE DISHONEST FOLK! HEH HEH HEH!
MEANWHILE...
WHAT'S GOOD ABOUT STEAM TRAINS IS THAT YOU CAN ALWAYS GET A HOT COFFEE... WHEN I WAS A STAGECOACH DRIVER...
HEY, LYNDON, I THINK THE BANDITS HAVE FINISHED...
ALREADY?... OK, GO AND TELL THE PASSENGERS TO LIFT THE TREE TRUNKS OFF THE TRACKS... AND TO DO IT A BIT QUICKER THAN DURING THE LAST ATTACK! I'VE NEVER SEEN A SOFTER BUNCH OF PASSENGERS THAN THOSE!
AND IF YOU'RE NOT HAPPY, WE'LL DISCONNECT THE LOCOMOTIVE AND CARRY ON ALONE. YOU'LL HAVE TO MAKE DO WITH THE WAGONS!
MORRIS GOSCINNY

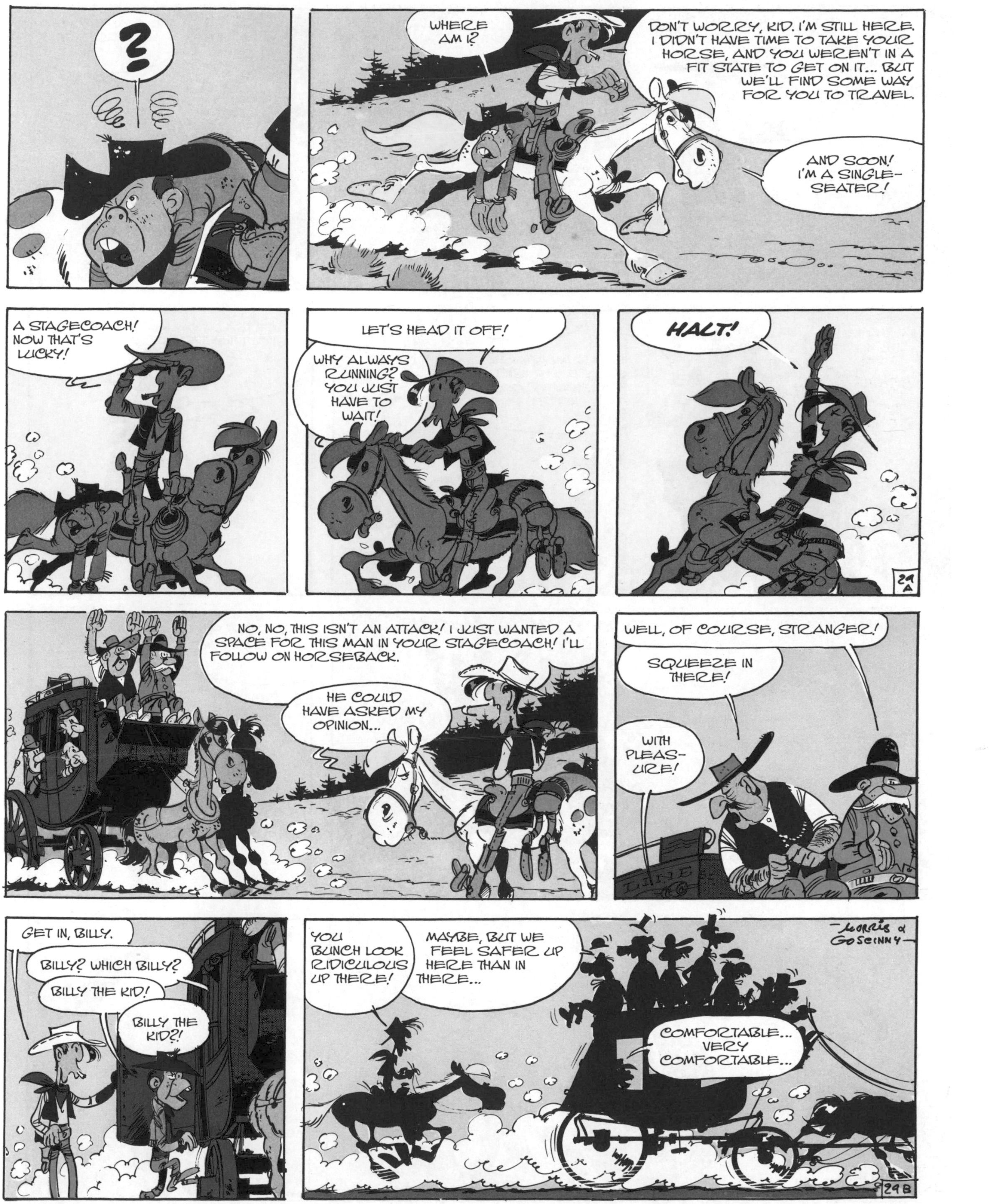
?
WHERE AM I?
DON'T WORRY, KID. I'M STILL HERE. I DIDN'T HAVE TIME TO TAKE YOUR HORSE, AND YOU WEREN'T IN A FIT STATE TO GET ON IT... BUT WE'LL FIND SOME WAY FOR YOU TO TRAVEL.
AND SOON! I'M A SINGLE-SEATER!
A STAGECOACH! NOW THAT'S LUCKY!
LET'S HEAD IT OFF!
WHY ALWAYS RUNNING? YOU JUST HAVE TO WAIT!
HALT!
NO, NO, THIS ISN'T AN ATTACK! I JUST WANTED A SPACE FOR THIS MAN IN YOUR STAGECOACH! I'LL FOLLOW ON HORSEBACK.
HE COULD HAVE ASKED MY OPINION...
WELL, OF COURSE, STRANGER!
SQUEEZE IN THERE!
WITH PLEASURE!
GET IN, BILLY.
BILLY? WHICH BILLY?
BILLY THE KID!
BILLY THE KID?!
YOU BUNCH LOOK RIDICULOUS UP THERE!
MAYBE, BUT WE FEEL SAFER UP HERE THAN IN THERE...
COMFORTABLE... VERY COMFORTABLE...
MORRIS & GOSCINNY

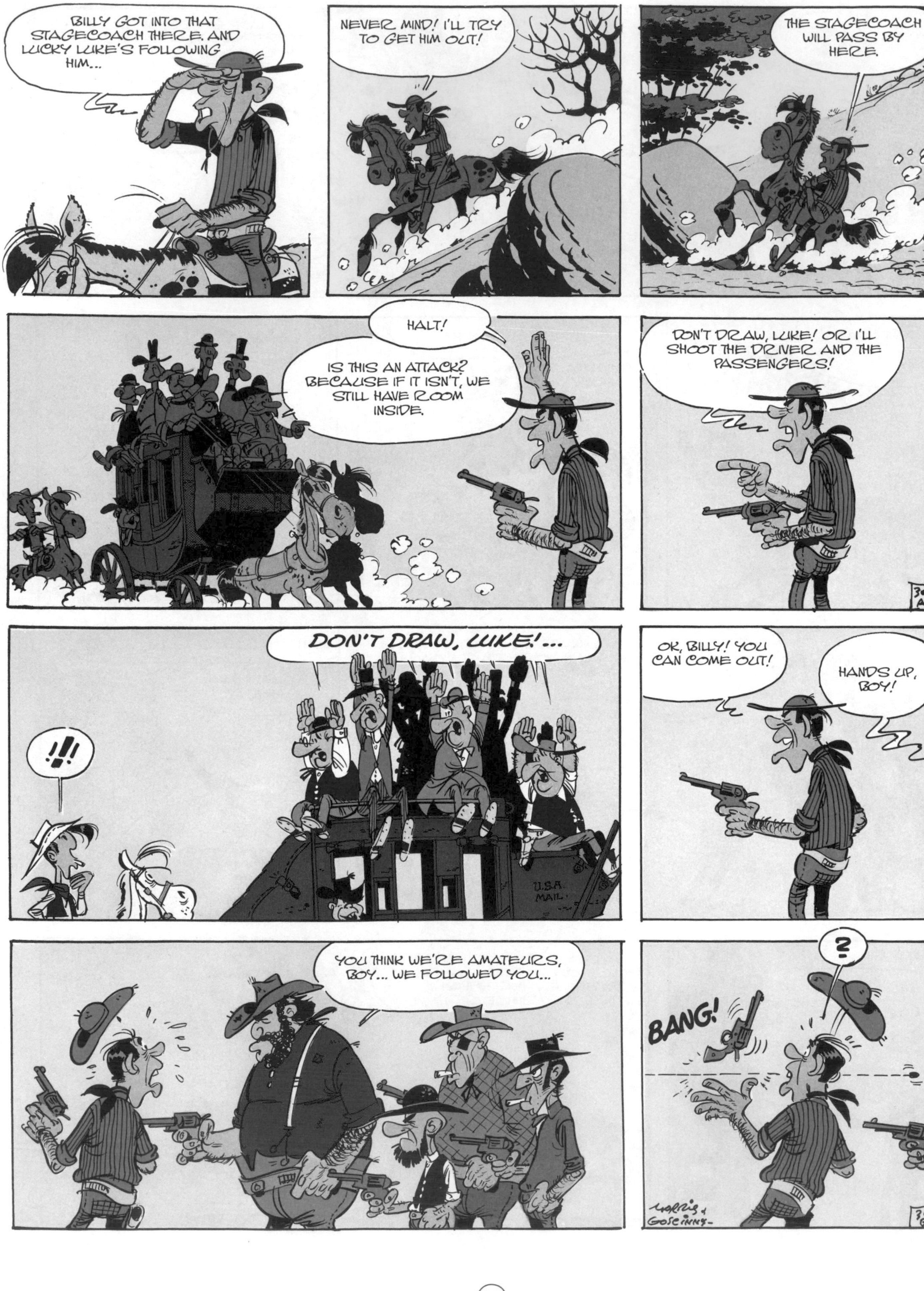
BILLY GOT INTO THAT STAGECOACH THERE, AND LUCKY LUKE'S FOLLOWING HIM...
NEVER MIND! I'LL TRY TO GET HIM OUT!
THE STAGECOACH WILL PASS BY HERE.
HALT!
IS THIS AN ATTACK? BECAUSE IF IT ISN'T, WE STILL HAVE ROOM INSIDE.
DON'T DRAW, LUKE! OR I'LL SHOOT THE DRIVER AND THE PASSENGERS!
30 A
DON'T DRAW, LUKE!...
!!!
U.S.A. MAIL
OK, BILLY! YOU CAN COME OUT!
HANDS UP, BOY!
YOU THINK WE'RE AMATEURS, BOY... WE FOLLOWED YOU...
?
BANG!
MORRIS & GOSCINNY
30 B

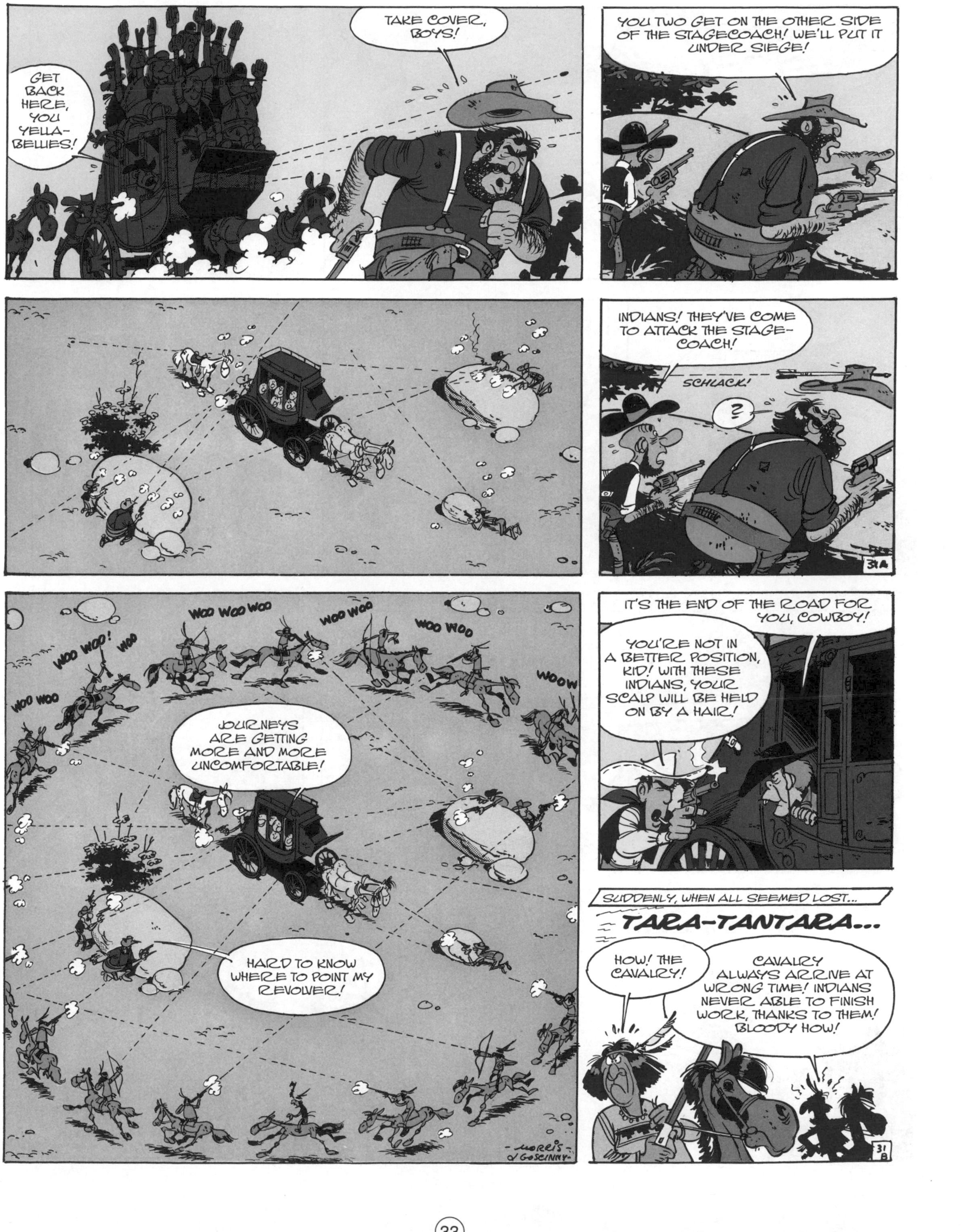
TAKE COVER, BOYS!
GET BACK HERE, YOU YELLA-BELLIES!
YOU TWO GET ON THE OTHER SIDE OF THE STAGECOACH! WE'LL PUT IT UNDER SIEGE!
INDIANS! THEY'VE COME TO ATTACK THE STAGE-COACH!
SCHLACK!
?
WOO WOO WOO
WOO WOO WOO
WOO WOO
WOO WOO! WOO
WOOW
WOO WOO
JOURNEYS ARE GETTING MORE AND MORE UNCOMFORTABLE!
HARD TO KNOW WHERE TO POINT MY REVOLVER!
IT'S THE END OF THE ROAD FOR YOU, COWBOY!
YOU'RE NOT IN A BETTER POSITION, KID! WITH THESE INDIANS, YOUR SCALP WILL BE HELD ON BY A HAIR!
SUDDENLY, WHEN ALL SEEMED LOST...
TARA-TANTARA...
HOW! THE CAVALRY!
CAVALRY ALWAYS ARRIVE AT WRONG TIME! INDIANS NEVER ABLE TO FINISH WORK, THANKS TO THEM! BLOODY HOW!
MORRIS GOSCINNY

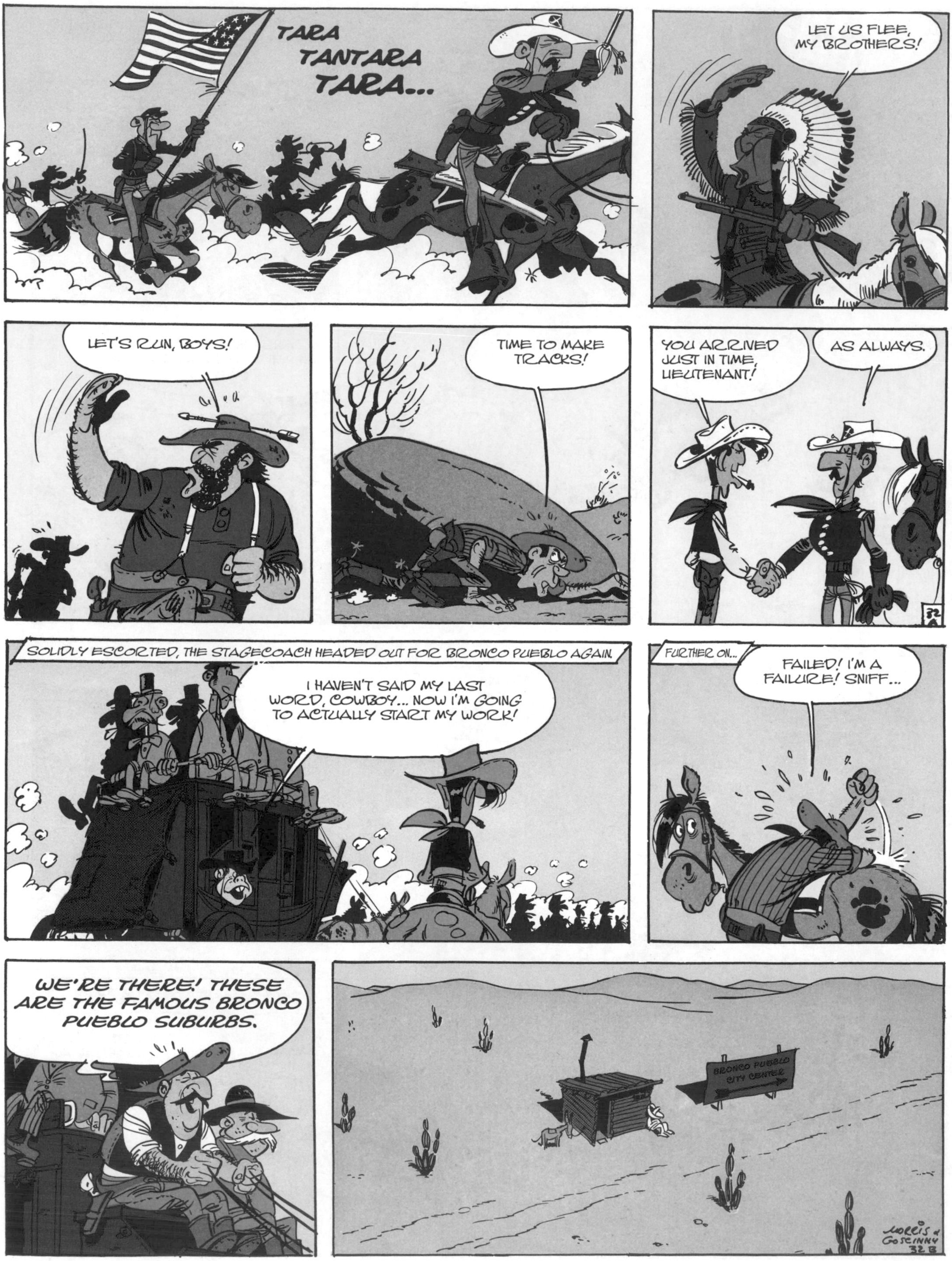
TARA TANTARA TARA...
LET US FLEE, MY BROTHERS!
LET'S RUN, BOYS!
TIME TO MAKE TRACKS!
YOU ARRIVED JUST IN TIME, LIEUTENANT!
AS ALWAYS.
SOLIDLY ESCORTED, THE STAGECOACH HEADED OUT FOR BRONCO PUEBLO AGAIN.
I HAVEN'T SAID MY LAST WORD, COWBOY... NOW I'M GOING TO ACTUALLY START MY WORK!
FURTHER ON...
FAILED! I'M A FAILURE! SNIFF...
WE'RE THERE! THESE ARE THE FAMOUS BRONCO PUEBLO SUBURBS.
BRONCO PUEBLO CITY CENTER

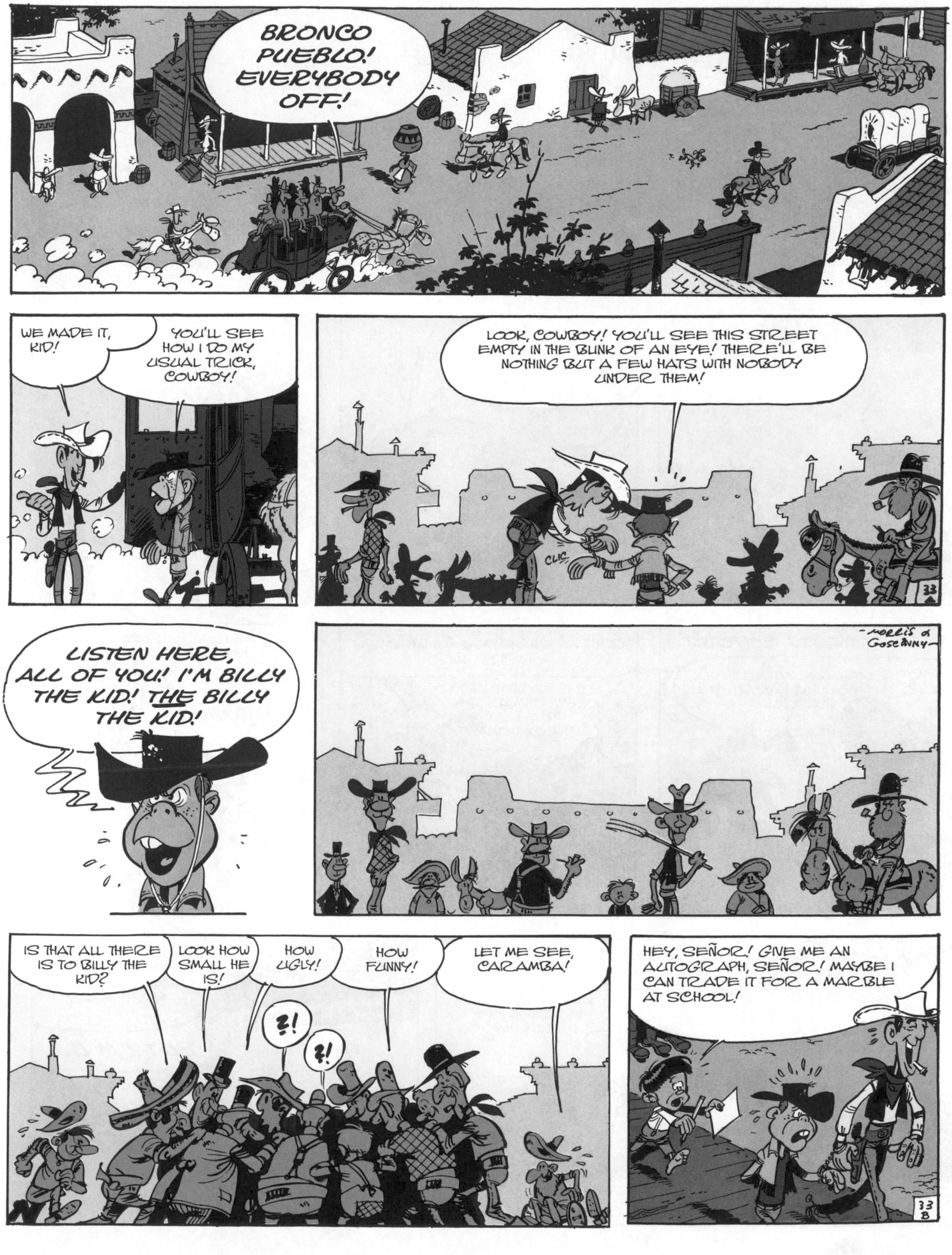
BRONCO PUEBLO! EVERYBODY OFF!
WE MADE IT, KID!
YOU'LL SEE HOW I DO MY USUAL TRICK, COWBOY!
LOOK, COWBOY! YOU'LL SEE THIS STREET EMPTY IN THE BLINK OF AN EYE! THERE'LL BE NOTHING BUT A FEW HATS WITH NOBODY UNDER THEM!
CLIC
LISTEN HERE, ALL OF YOU! I'M BILLY THE KID! THE BILLY THE KID!
IS THAT ALL THERE IS TO BILLY THE KID?
LOOK HOW SMALL HE IS!
HOW UGLY!
HOW FUNNY!
LET ME SEE, CARAMBA!
?!
?!
HEY, SEÑOR! GIVE ME AN AUTOGRAPH, SEÑOR! MAYBE I CAN TRADE IT FOR A MARBLE AT SCHOOL!

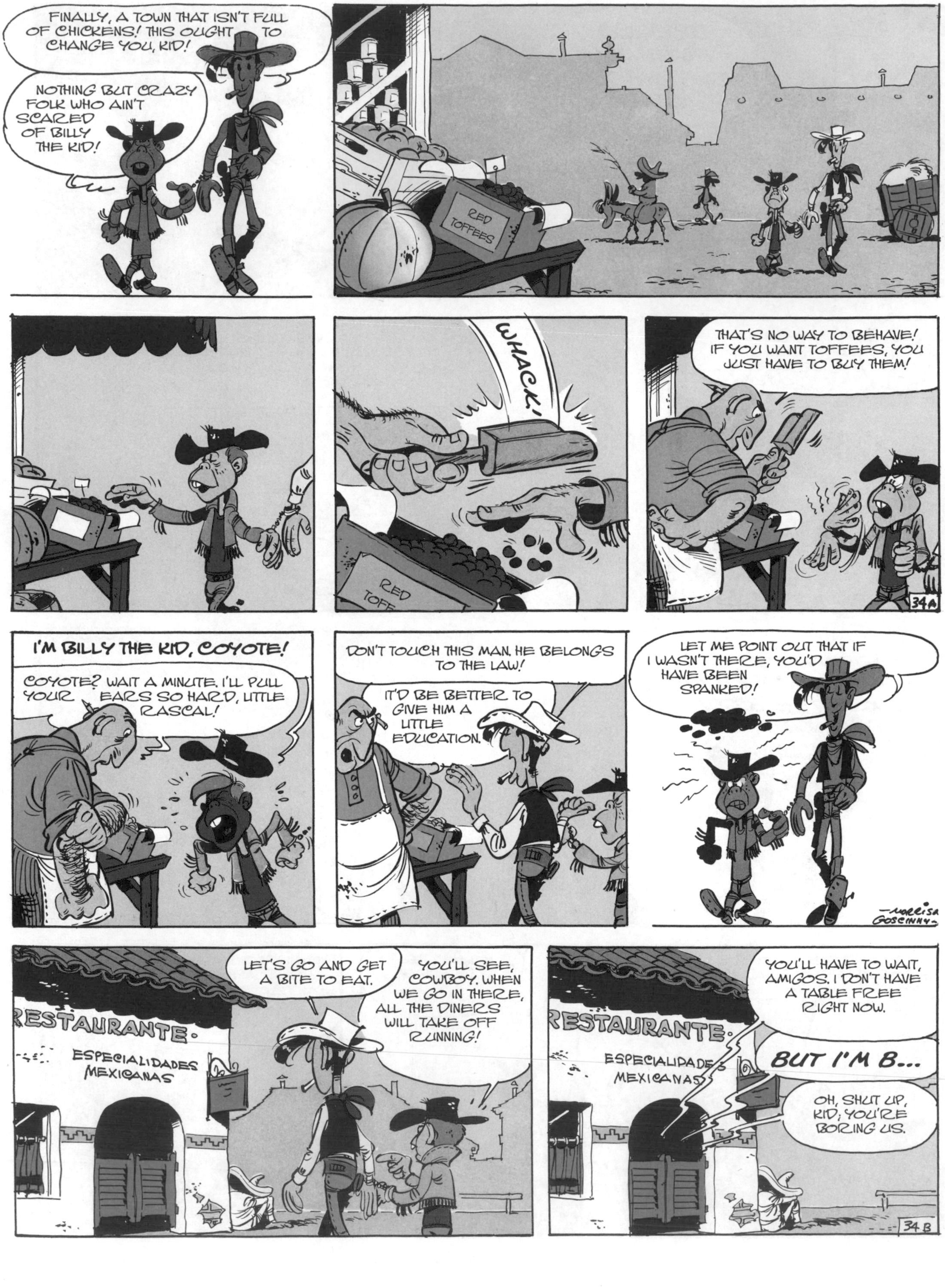

FINALLY, A TOWN THAT ISN'T FULL OF CHICKENS! THIS OUGHT TO CHANGE YOU, KID!
NOTHING BUT CRAZY FOLK WHO AIN'T SCARED OF BILLY THE KID!
RED TOFFEES
WHACK!
THAT'S NO WAY TO BEHAVE! IF YOU WANT TOFFEES, YOU JUST HAVE TO BUY THEM!
34A
I'M BILLY THE KID, COYOTE!
COYOTE? WAIT A MINUTE. I'LL PULL YOUR EARS SO HARD, LITTLE RASCAL!
DON'T TOUCH THIS MAN. HE BELONGS TO THE LAW!
IT'D BE BETTER TO GIVE HIM A LITTLE EDUCATION.
LET ME POINT OUT THAT IF I WASN'T THERE, YOU'D HAVE BEEN SPANKED!
MORRIS & GOSCINNY
LET'S GO AND GET A BITE TO EAT.
YOU'LL SEE, COWBOY. WHEN WE GO IN THERE, ALL THE DINERS WILL TAKE OFF RUNNING!
RESTAURANTE
ESPECIALIDADES MEXICANAS
YOU'LL HAVE TO WAIT, AMIGOS. I DON'T HAVE A TABLE FREE RIGHT NOW.
BUT I'M B...
OH, SHUT UP, KID; YOU'RE BORING US.
34B

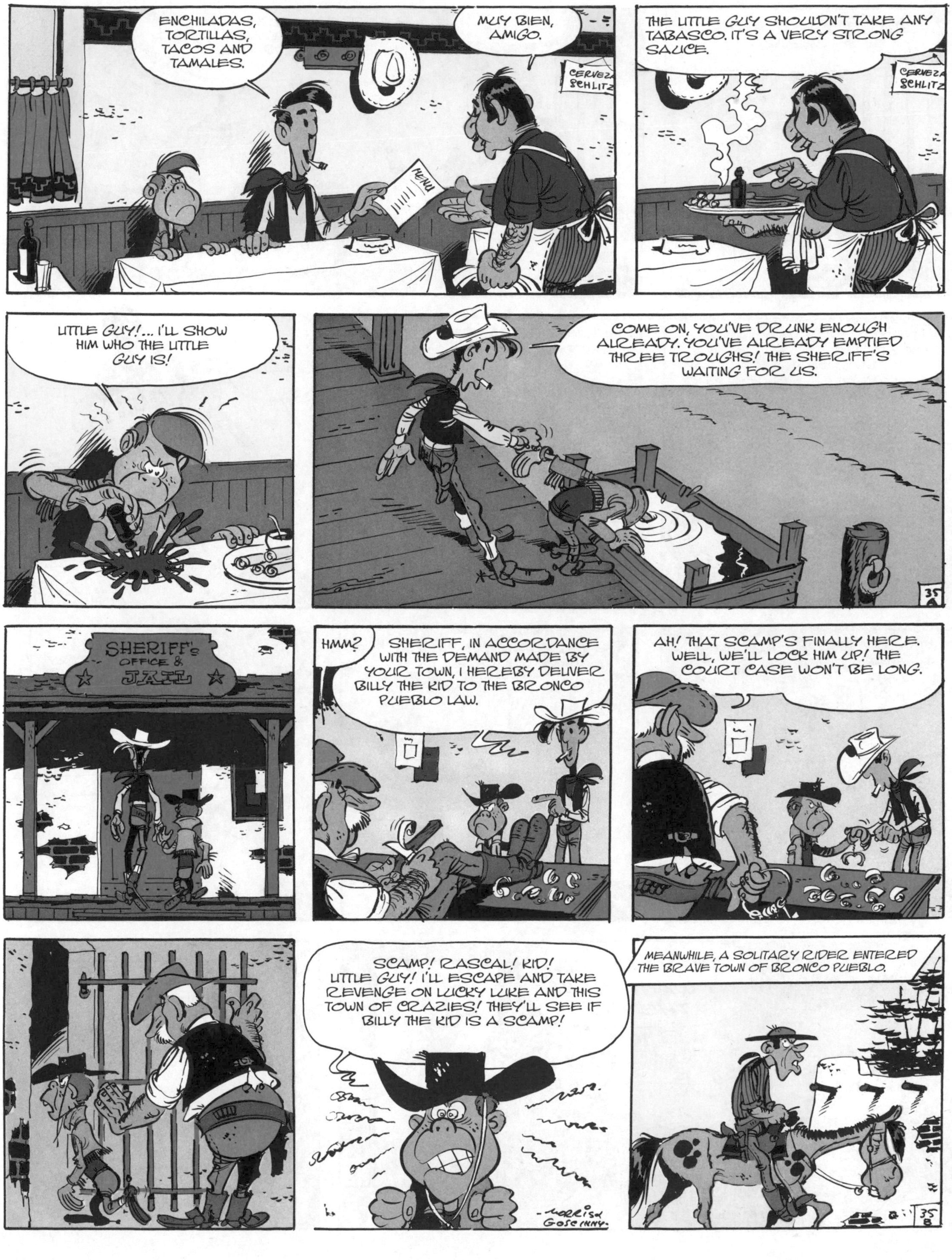
ENCHILADAS, TORTILLAS, TACOS AND TAMALES.
MUY BIEN, AMIGO.
CERVEZA SCHLITZ
MENU
THE LITTLE GUY SHOULDN'T TAKE ANY TABASCO. IT'S A VERY STRONG SAUCE.
CERVEZA SCHLITZ
LITTLE GUY!... I'LL SHOW HIM WHO THE LITTLE GUY IS!
COME ON, YOU'VE DRUNK ENOUGH ALREADY. YOU'VE ALREADY EMPTIED THREE TROUGHS! THE SHERIFF'S WAITING FOR US.
35 A
SHERIFF's OFFICE & JAIL
HMM?
SHERIFF, IN ACCORDANCE WITH THE DEMAND MADE BY YOUR TOWN, I HEREBY DELIVER BILLY THE KID TO THE BRONCO PUEBLO LAW.
AH! THAT SCAMP'S FINALLY HERE. WELL, WE'LL LOCK HIM UP! THE COURT CASE WON'T BE LONG.
SCAMP! RASCAL! KID! LITTLE GUY! I'LL ESCAPE AND TAKE REVENGE ON LUCKY LUKE AND THIS TOWN OF CRAZIES! THEY'LL SEE IF BILLY THE KID IS A SCAMP!
MORRIS GOSCINNY
MEANWHILE, A SOLITARY RIDER ENTERED THE BRAVE TOWN OF BRONCO PUEBLO.
35 B

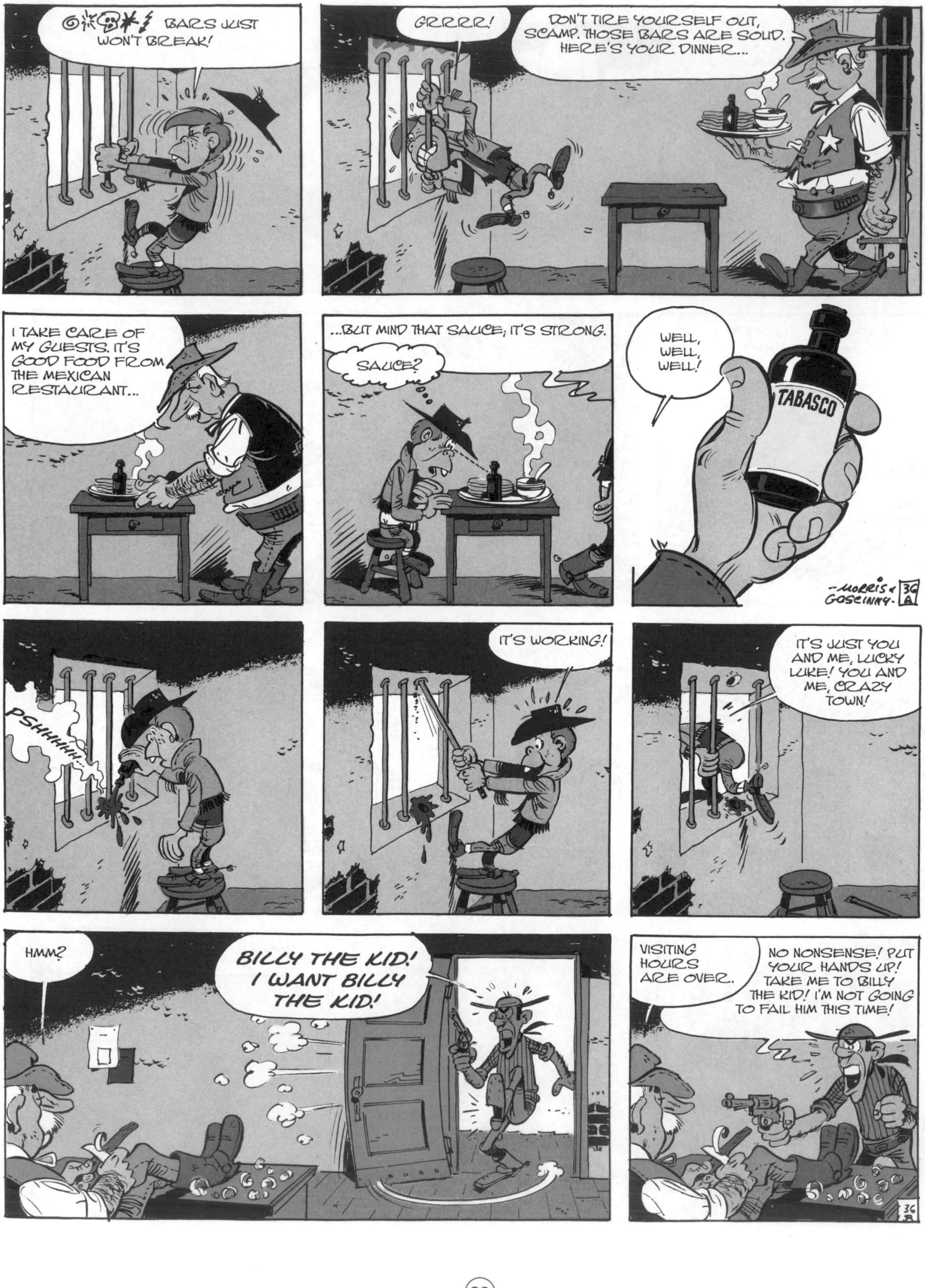

@*!☠*! BARS JUST WON'T BREAK!
GRRRR!
DON'T TIRE YOURSELF OUT, SCAMP. THOSE BARS ARE SOLID. HERE'S YOUR DINNER...
I TAKE CARE OF MY GUESTS. IT'S GOOD FOOD FROM THE MEXICAN RESTAURANT...
...BUT MIND THAT SAUCE; IT'S STRONG.
SAUCE?
WELL, WELL, WELL!
TABASCO
MORRIS & GOSCINNY
36 A
PSHHHHH!
IT'S WORKING!
IT'S JUST YOU AND ME, LUCKY LUKE! YOU AND ME, CRAZY TOWN!
HMM?
BILLY THE KID! I WANT BILLY THE KID!
VISITING HOURS ARE OVER.
NO NONSENSE! PUT YOUR HANDS UP! TAKE ME TO BILLY THE KID! I'M NOT GOING TO FAIL HIM THIS TIME!
36 B

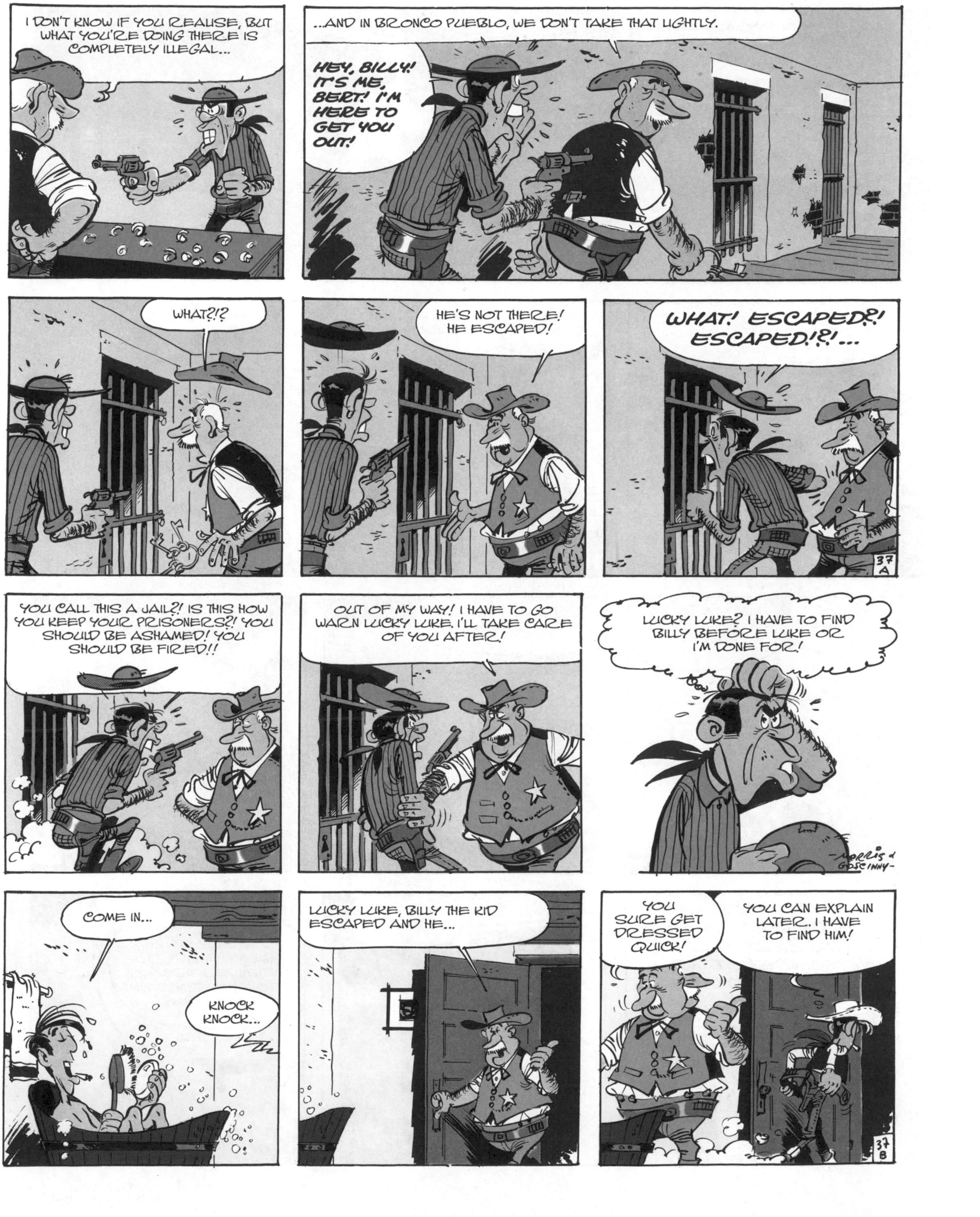

I DON'T KNOW IF YOU REALISE, BUT WHAT YOU'RE DOING THERE IS COMPLETELY ILLEGAL...
...AND IN BRONCO PUEBLO, WE DON'T TAKE THAT LIGHTLY.
HEY, BILLY! IT'S ME, BERT! I'M HERE TO GET YOU OUT!
WHAT?!?
HE'S NOT THERE! HE ESCAPED!
WHAT! ESCAPED?! ESCAPED!?!...
37 A
YOU CALL THIS A JAIL?! IS THIS HOW YOU KEEP YOUR PRISONERS?! YOU SHOULD BE ASHAMED! YOU SHOULD BE FIRED!!
OUT OF MY WAY! I HAVE TO GO WARN LUCKY LUKE. I'LL TAKE CARE OF YOU AFTER!
LUCKY LUKE? I HAVE TO FIND BILLY BEFORE LUKE OR I'M DONE FOR!
MORRIS & GOSCINNY
COME IN...
KNOCK KNOCK...
LUCKY LUKE, BILLY THE KID ESCAPED AND HE...
YOU SURE GET DRESSED QUICK!
YOU CAN EXPLAIN LATER.. I HAVE TO FIND HIM!
37 B

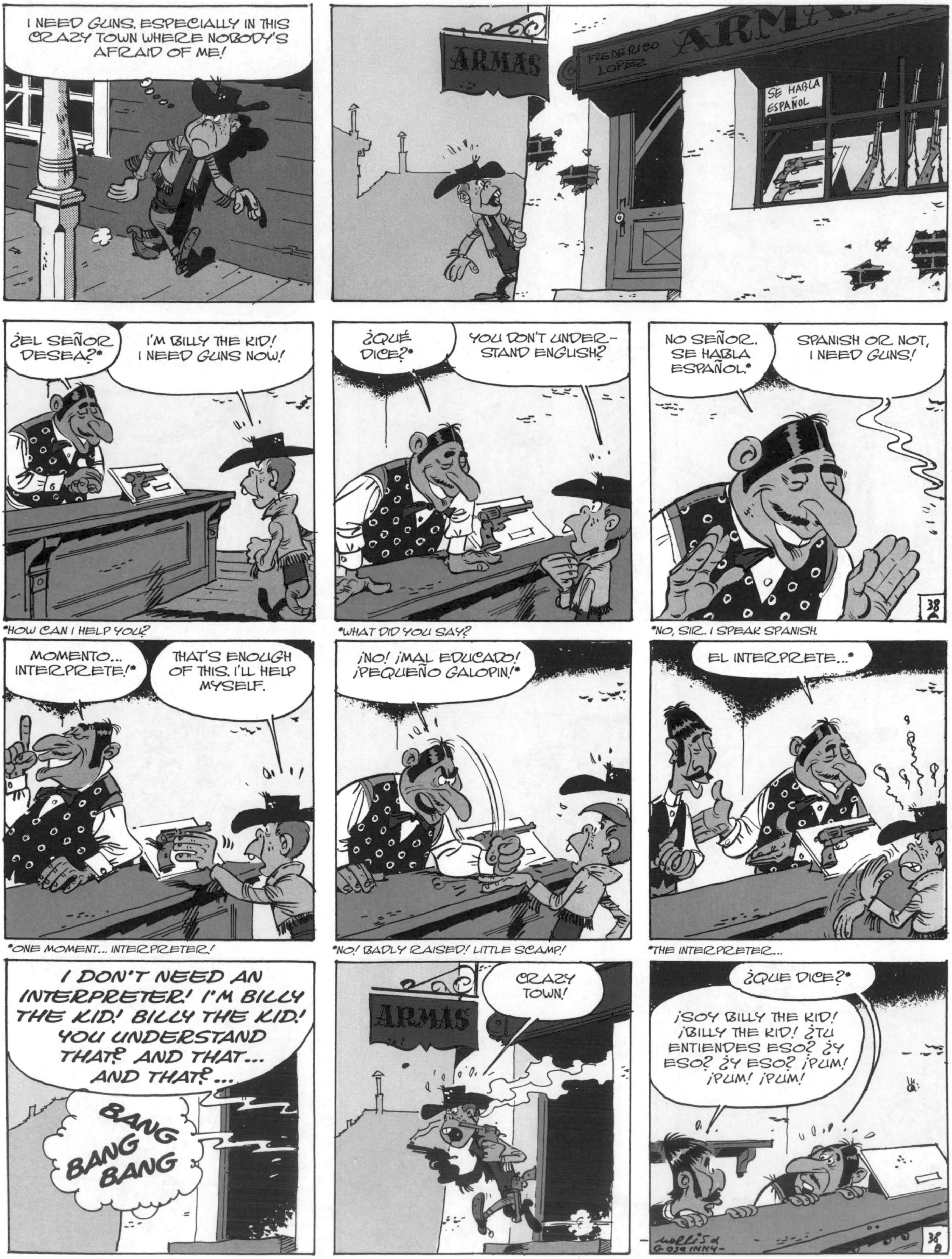
I NEED GUNS. ESPECIALLY IN THIS CRAZY TOWN WHERE NOBODY'S AFRAID OF ME!
ARMAS
FREDERICO LOPEZ
ARMAS
SE HABLA ESPAÑOL
¿EL SEÑOR DESEA?*
I'M BILLY THE KID! I NEED GUNS NOW!
¿QUÉ DICE?*
YOU DON'T UNDERSTAND ENGLISH?
NO SEÑOR. SE HABLA ESPAÑOL.*
SPANISH OR NOT, I NEED GUNS!
MOMENTO... INTERPRETE!*
THAT'S ENOUGH OF THIS. I'LL HELP MYSELF.
¡NO! ¡MAL EDUCADO! ¡PEQUEÑO GALOPIN!*
EL INTERPRETE...*
I DON'T NEED AN INTERPRETER! I'M BILLY THE KID! BILLY THE KID! YOU UNDERSTAND THAT? AND THAT... AND THAT?...
BANG BANG BANG
ARMAS
CRAZY TOWN!
¿QUE DICE?*
¡SOY BILLY THE KID! ¡BILLY THE KID! ¿TU ENTIENDES ESO? ¿Y ESO? ¿Y ESO? ¡PUM! ¡PUM! ¡PUM!

*HOW CAN I HELP YOU?

*WHAT DID YOU SAY?

*NO, SIR. I SPEAK SPANISH.

*ONE MOMENT... INTERPRETER!

*NO! BADLY RAISED! LITTLE SCAMP!

*THE INTERPRETER...

*WHAT DID HE SAY?
*I'M BILLY THE KID! BILLY THE KID! YOU UNDERSTAND THAT? AND THAT? AND THAT? BANG! BANG! BANG!

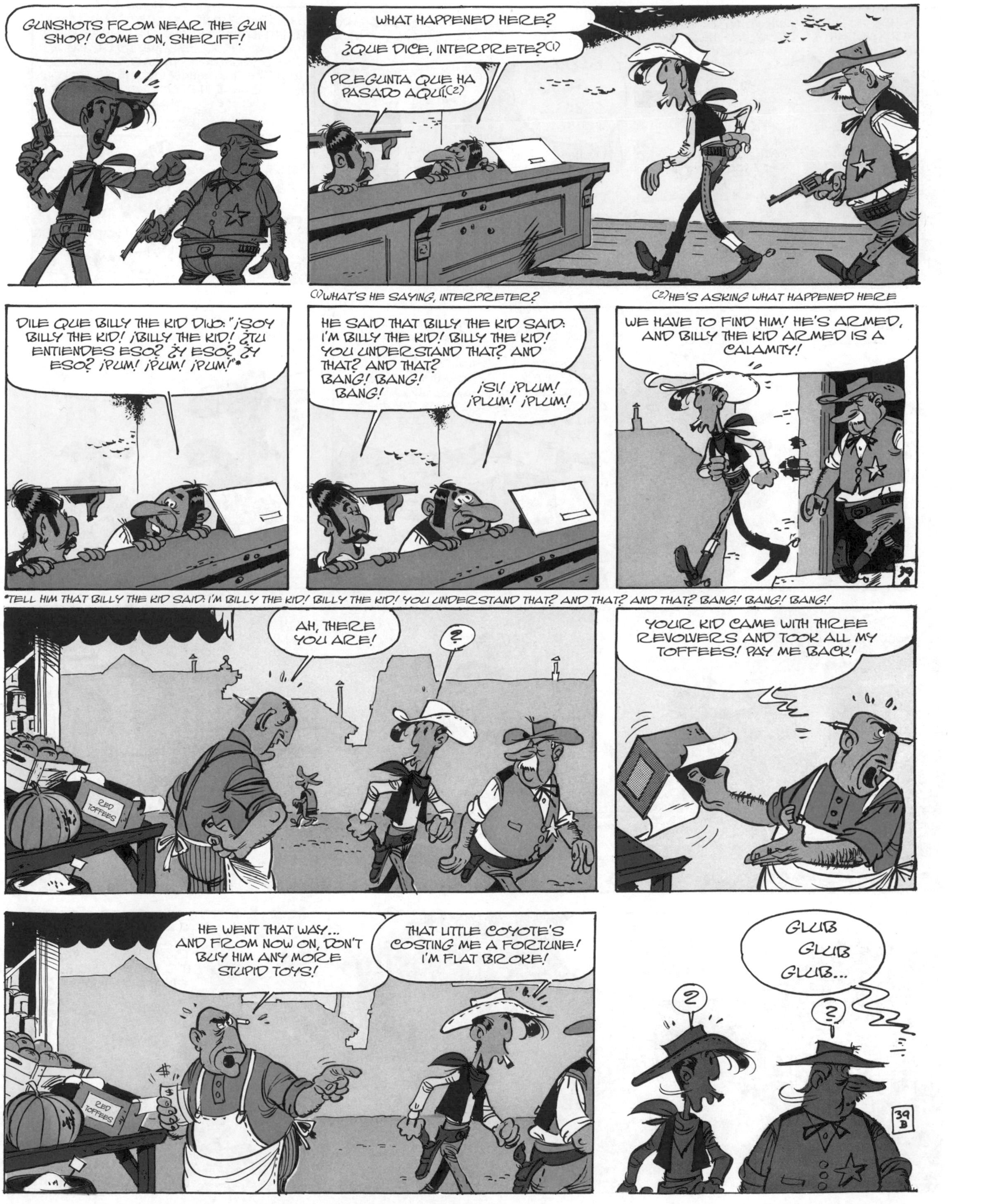
GUNSHOTS FROM NEAR THE GUN SHOP! COME ON, SHERIFF!
WHAT HAPPENED HERE?
¿QUE DICE, INTERPRETE?(1)
PREGUNTA QUE HA PASADO AQUÍ.(2)
(1) WHAT'S HE SAYING, INTERPRETER?
(2) HE'S ASKING WHAT HAPPENED HERE
DILE QUE BILLY THE KID DIJO: "¡SOY BILLY THE KID! ¡BILLY THE KID! ¿TU ENTIENDES ESO? ¿Y ESO? ¿Y ESO? ¡PUM! ¡PUM! ¡PUM!"*
HE SAID THAT BILLY THE KID SAID: I'M BILLY THE KID! BILLY THE KID! YOU UNDERSTAND THAT? AND THAT? AND THAT? BANG! BANG! BANG!
¡SI! ¡PLUM! ¡PLUM! ¡PLUM!
WE HAVE TO FIND HIM! HE'S ARMED, AND BILLY THE KID ARMED IS A CALAMITY!
*TELL HIM THAT BILLY THE KID SAID: I'M BILLY THE KID! BILLY THE KID! YOU UNDERSTAND THAT? AND THAT? AND THAT? BANG! BANG! BANG!
AH, THERE YOU ARE!
?
RED TOFFEES
YOUR KID CAME WITH THREE REVOLVERS AND TOOK ALL MY TOFFEES! PAY ME BACK!
HE WENT THAT WAY... AND FROM NOW ON, DON'T BUY HIM ANY MORE STUPID TOYS!
THAT LITTLE COYOTE'S COSTING ME A FORTUNE! I'M FLAT BROKE!
RED TOFFEES
GLUB GLUB GLUB...
?
?

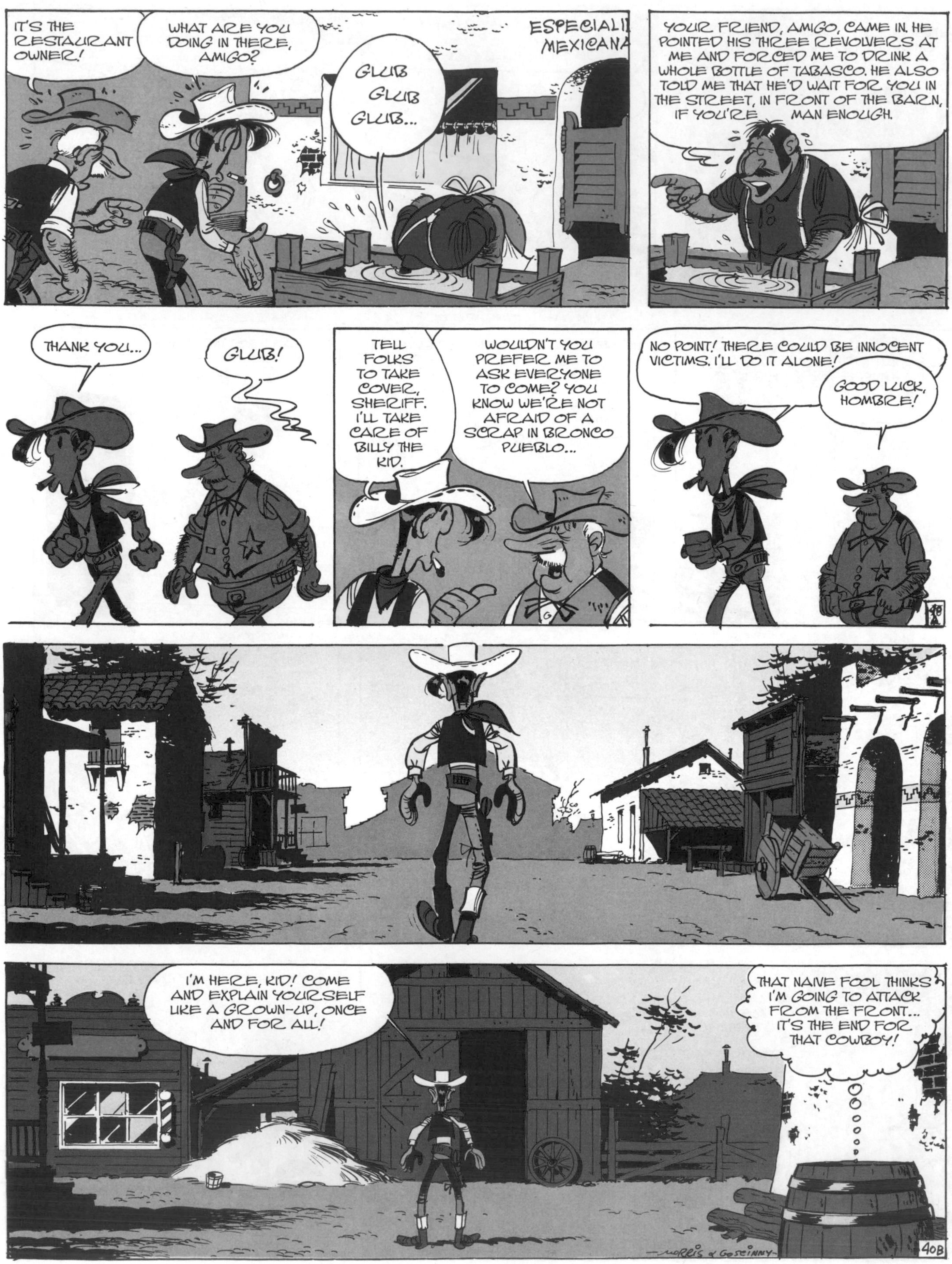
IT'S THE RESTAURANT OWNER!
WHAT ARE YOU DOING IN THERE, AMIGO?
ESPECIALI MEXICANA
GLUB GLUB GLUB...
YOUR FRIEND, AMIGO, CAME IN. HE POINTED HIS THREE REVOLVERS AT ME AND FORCED ME TO DRINK A WHOLE BOTTLE OF TABASCO. HE ALSO TOLD ME THAT HE'D WAIT FOR YOU IN THE STREET, IN FRONT OF THE BARN, IF YOU'RE MAN ENOUGH.
THANK YOU...
GLUB!
TELL FOLKS TO TAKE COVER, SHERIFF. I'LL TAKE CARE OF BILLY THE KID.
WOULDN'T YOU PREFER ME TO ASK EVERYONE TO COME? YOU KNOW WE'RE NOT AFRAID OF A SCRAP IN BRONCO PUEBLO...
NO POINT! THERE COULD BE INNOCENT VICTIMS. I'LL DO IT ALONE!
GOOD LUCK, HOMBRE!
I'M HERE, KID! COME AND EXPLAIN YOURSELF LIKE A GROWN-UP, ONCE AND FOR ALL!
THAT NAIVE FOOL THINKS I'M GOING TO ATTACK FROM THE FRONT... IT'S THE END FOR THAT COWBOY!
MORRIS & GOSCINNY
40B

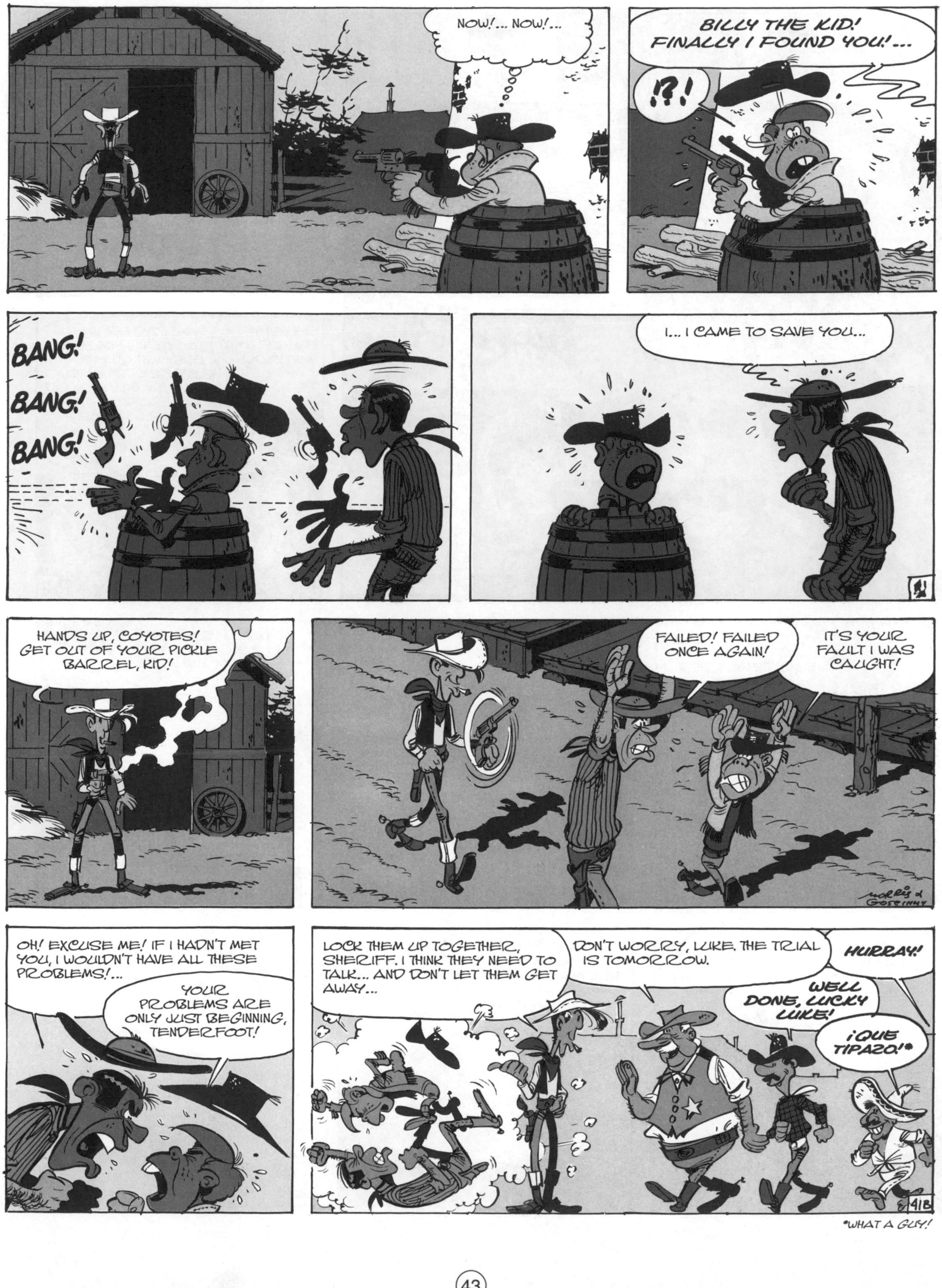
NOW!... NOW!...
BILLY THE KID! FINALLY I FOUND YOU!...
!?!
BANG!
BANG!
BANG!
I... I CAME TO SAVE YOU...
HANDS UP, COYOTES! GET OUT OF YOUR PICKLE BARREL, KID!
FAILED! FAILED ONCE AGAIN!
IT'S YOUR FAULT I WAS CAUGHT!
MORRIS & GOSCINNY
OH! EXCUSE ME! IF I HADN'T MET YOU, I WOULDN'T HAVE ALL THESE PROBLEMS!...
YOUR PROBLEMS ARE ONLY JUST BEGINNING, TENDERFOOT!
LOCK THEM UP TOGETHER, SHERIFF. I THINK THEY NEED TO TALK... AND DON'T LET THEM GET AWAY...
DON'T WORRY, LUKE. THE TRIAL IS TOMORROW.
HURRAY!
WELL DONE, LUCKY LUKE!
¡QUE TIPAZO!*

*WHAT A GUY!

SILENCE IN THE COURTROOM! THIS COURT IS IN SESSION. THE TERRITORY OF NEW MEXICO AGAINST WILLIAM H. BONNEY, KNOWN AS BILLY THE KID. THE PROSECUTOR HAS THE STAND.

BEFORE BEING CONDEMNED TO 1,247 YEARS OF PRISON IN ANOTHER STATE FOR OTHER CRIMES, BILLY THE KID CAME TO BRONCO PUEBLO. HE TETHERED HIS HORSE IN FRONT OF THE SALOON, IN A NO-PARKING ZONE...

SHERIFF, TELL US WHAT YOU KNOW.

I ORDERED BILLY TO PUT HIS HORSE ELSEWHERE. HE REFUSED TO OBEY, SAYING, "I'M BILLY THE KID, AND MY HORSE WILL STAY HERE FOR AS LONG AS I WANT IT TO."

MY CLIENT PLEADS GUILTY AND ASKS FOR THE JURY'S LENIENCY.

THE JURY FOUND HIM GUILTY ON ALL COUNTS.

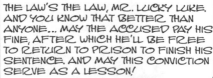

WILLIAM H. BONNEY, YOU'RE CONDEMNED TO A $5 FINE!

AND THAT'S WHAT I JUST CAME HUNDREDS OF MILES FOR?!

THE LAW'S THE LAW, MR. LUCKY LUKE, AND YOU KNOW THAT BETTER THAN ANYONE... MAY THE ACCUSED PAY HIS FINE, AFTER WHICH HE'LL BE FREE TO RETURN TO PRISON TO FINISH HIS SENTENCE. AND MAY THIS CONVICTION SERVE AS A LESSON!

I WANT TO PAY MY FINE, BUT I HAVEN'T GOT ANY MONEY ON ME... GIVE ME FIVE MINUTES, JUST LONG ENOUGH TO HOLD UP A BANK.

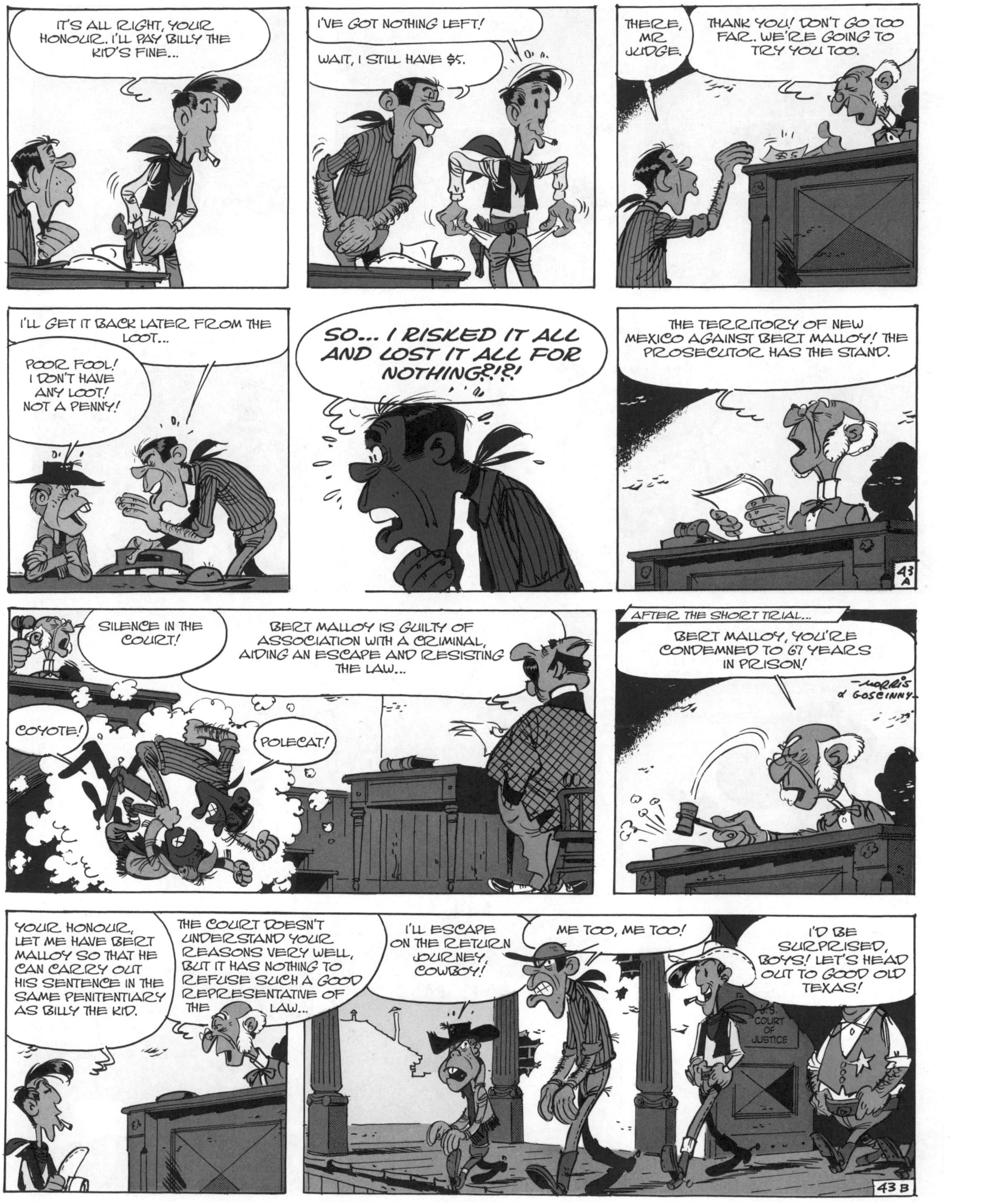
IT'S ALL RIGHT, YOUR HONOUR. I'LL PAY BILLY THE KID'S FINE...
I'VE GOT NOTHING LEFT!
WAIT, I STILL HAVE $5.
THERE, MR JUDGE.
$5
THANK YOU! DON'T GO TOO FAR. WE'RE GOING TO TRY YOU TOO.
I'LL GET IT BACK LATER FROM THE LOOT...
POOR FOOL! I DON'T HAVE ANY LOOT! NOT A PENNY!
SO... I RISKED IT ALL AND LOST IT ALL FOR NOTHING?!?!
THE TERRITORY OF NEW MEXICO AGAINST BERT MALLOY! THE PROSECUTOR HAS THE STAND.
43 A
SILENCE IN THE COURT!
BERT MALLOY IS GUILTY OF ASSOCIATION WITH A CRIMINAL, AIDING AN ESCAPE AND RESISTING THE LAW...
COYOTE!
POLECAT!
AFTER THE SHORT TRIAL...
BERT MALLOY, YOU'RE CONDEMNED TO 67 YEARS IN PRISON!
MORRIS & GOSCINNY
YOUR HONOUR, LET ME HAVE BERT MALLOY SO THAT HE CAN CARRY OUT HIS SENTENCE IN THE SAME PENITENTIARY AS BILLY THE KID.
THE COURT DOESN'T UNDERSTAND YOUR REASONS VERY WELL, BUT IT HAS NOTHING TO REFUSE SUCH A GOOD REPRESENTATIVE OF THE LAW...
I'LL ESCAPE ON THE RETURN JOURNEY, COWBOY!
ME TOO, ME TOO!
I'D BE SURPRISED, BOYS! LET'S HEAD OUT TO GOOD OLD TEXAS!
U.S. COURT OF JUSTICE
43 B

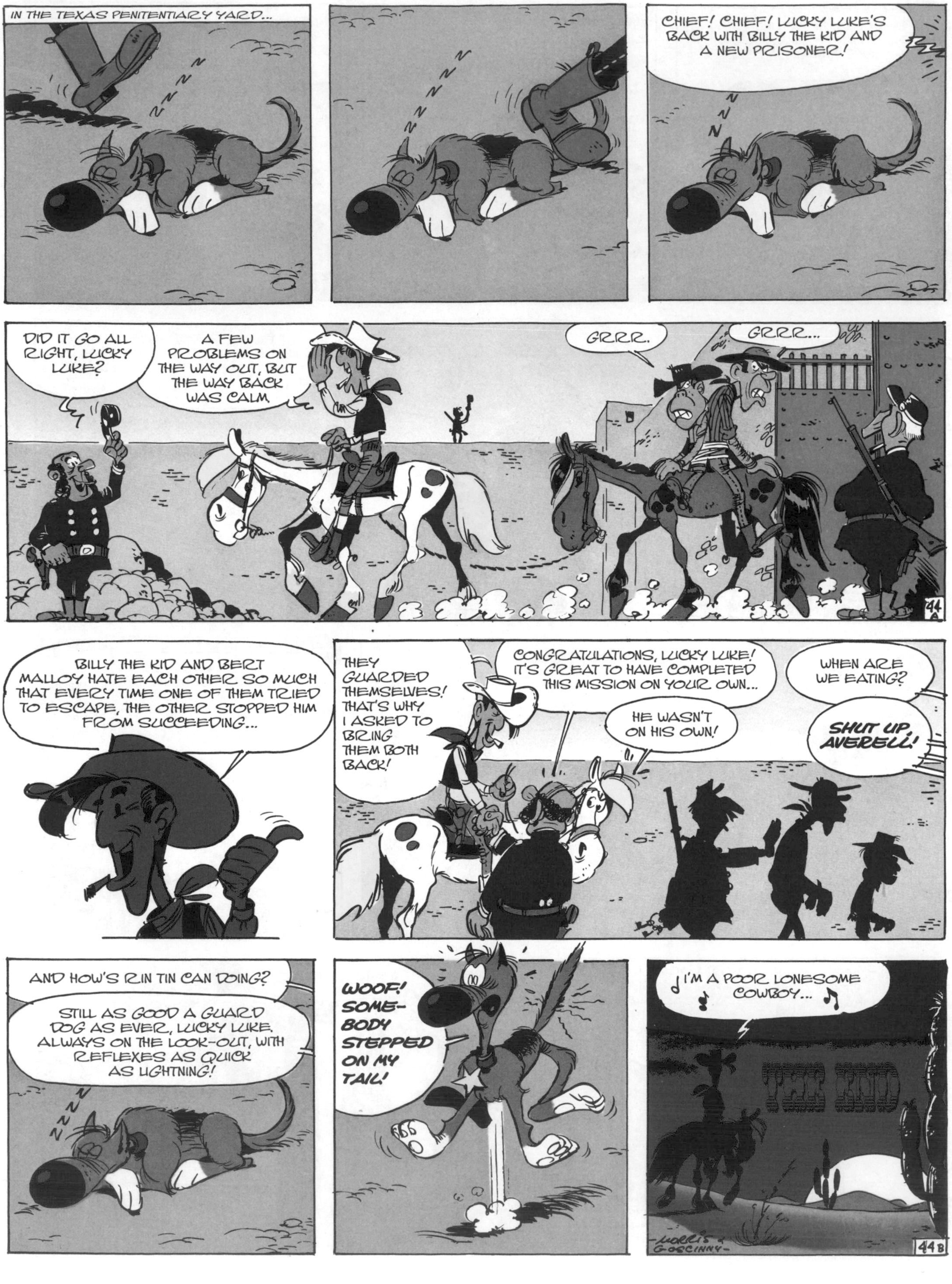
IN THE TEXAS PENITENTIARY YARD...
Z
Z
Z
Z
Z
Z
CHIEF! CHIEF! LUCKY LUKE'S BACK WITH BILLY THE KID AND A NEW PRISONER!
Z
Z
Z
DID IT GO ALL RIGHT, LUCKY LUKE?
A FEW PROBLEMS ON THE WAY OUT, BUT THE WAY BACK WAS CALM.
GRRR.
GRRR...
44 A
BILLY THE KID AND BERT MALLOY HATE EACH OTHER SO MUCH THAT EVERY TIME ONE OF THEM TRIED TO ESCAPE, THE OTHER STOPPED HIM FROM SUCCEEDING...
THEY GUARDED THEMSELVES! THAT'S WHY I ASKED TO BRING THEM BOTH BACK!
CONGRATULATIONS, LUCKY LUKE! IT'S GREAT TO HAVE COMPLETED THIS MISSION ON YOUR OWN...
HE WASN'T ON HIS OWN!
WHEN ARE WE EATING?
SHUT UP, AVERELL!
AND HOW'S RIN TIN CAN DOING?
STILL AS GOOD A GUARD DOG AS EVER, LUCKY LUKE. ALWAYS ON THE LOOK-OUT, WITH REFLEXES AS QUICK AS LIGHTNING!
Z
Z
Z
WOOF! SOME-BODY STEPPED ON MY TAIL!
I'M A POOR LONESOME COWBOY...
THE END
MORRIS & GOSCINNY
44 B

9th CINEBOOK
The 9th Art Publisher
presents

LUCKY LUKE

The man who shoots faster than his own shadow

A LUCKY LUKE ADVENTURE 1
BILLY the Kid
MORRIS & GOSCINNY
CINEBOOK

A LUCKY LUKE ADVENTURE 2
GHOST TOWN
MORRIS & GOSCINNY
CINEBOOK

A LUCKY LUKE ADVENTURE 3
DALTON CITY
MORRIS & GOSCINNY
CINEBOOK

A LUCKY LUKE ADVENTURE 4
JESSE JAMES
MORRIS & GOSCINNY
CINEBOOK

A LUCKY LUKE ADVENTURE 5
IN THE SHADOW OF THE DERRICKS
E.L. DRAKE OIL CO.
MORRIS & GOSCINNY
CINEBOOK

A LUCKY LUKE ADVENTURE 6
MA DALTON
MORRIS & GOSCINNY
WANTED
DALTON brothers
CINEBOOK

A LUCKY LUKE ADVENTURE 7
BARBED WIRE ON THE PRAIRIE
MORRIS & GOSCINNY
CINEBOOK

A LUCKY LUKE ADVENTURE 8
CALAMITY JANE
MORRIS & GOSCINNY
CINEBOOK

A LUCKY LUKE ADVENTURE 9
THE WAGON TRAIN
MORRIS & GOSCINNY
CINEBOOK

A LUCKY LUKE ADVENTURE 10
TORTILLAS FOR THE DALTONS
MORRIS & GOSCINNY
CINEBOOK

A LUCKY LUKE ADVENTURE 11
WESTERN CIRCUS
MORRIS & GOSCINNY
CINEBOOK

A LUCKY LUKE ADVENTURE 12
THE RIVALS OF PAINFUL GULCH
MORRIS & GOSCINNY
CINEBOOK

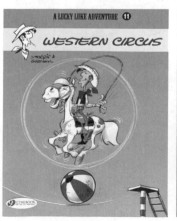

A LUCKY LUKE ADVENTURE 13
THE TENDERFOOT
MORRIS & GOSCINNY

A LUCKY LUKE ADVENTURE 14
THE DASHING WHITE COWBOY
CINEBOOK

A LUCKY LUKE ADVENTURE 15
THE DALTONS IN THE BLIZZARD
CINEBOOK

A LUCKY LUKE ADVENTURE 16
THE BLACK HILLS
CINEBOOK

COMING SOON

A LUCKY LUKE ADVENTURE 17
APACHE CANYON
MORRIS & GOSCINNY
CINEBOOK

A LUCKY LUKE ADVENTURE 18
THE ESCORT
CINEBOOK

A LUCKY LUKE ADVENTURE 19
ON THE DALTONS' TRAIL
CINEBOOK

A LUCKY LUKE ADVENTURE 20
THE OKLAHOMA LAND RUSH
CINEBOOK

OCTOBER 2009

DECEMBER 2009

A LUCKY LUKE ADVENTURE 21
THE 20TH CAVALRY
CINEBOOK

A LUCKY LUKE ADVENTURE 22
EMPEROR SMITH
CINEBOOK

A LUCKY LUKE ADVENTURE 23
A CURE FOR THE DALTONS
CINEBOOK

A LUCKY LUKE ADVENTURE 24
THE JUDGE
BEER
WITNESS
ACCUSED
CINEBOOK

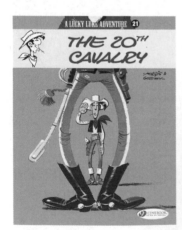

FEBRUARY 2010

APRIL 2010

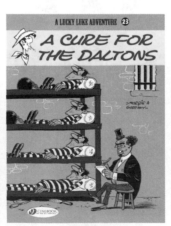

JUNE 2010

AUGUST 2010

CINEBOOK
The 9th Art Publisher
www.cinebook.com